DREAM MIRE

A Woodsdale Novel

By Sharman Badgett-Young

Available in e-book edition from
Amazon (in multiple countries).
ASIN: B01L4J0UNC

Available in trade paperback from
createspace.com/5655115
ISBN-10: 1515337642
ISBN-13: 978-1515337645

For those who live
with the stigma of mental illness.

Mire *noun* [ˈmī(ə)r]

1. Swamp or bog; soft, squishy mud
2. A problematic or discomforting situation from which it is difficult to escape.

Chapter 1

The thing is, I never expected to make it this far.

* * *

I nab the last open table in the public library, and mentally applaud. The air tickling my nose carries the familiar dust of decades, and I grin. This is my place.

At the next table, two middle-aged men have descended into fervent discussion at non-quiet-zone levels. Yuck. No wonder mine's the last open table. I press in earbuds to block their clamor.

Out of my daypack, I dump the first cut of sources from my University of Washington advisor. Determined to take control of it, I let my blues stare down the books, journals, and online resource lists. I'm in charge here.

The heap aims to steal my summer vacation. But honestly, I chose it. If I complete the background research for my doctoral dissertation before September, I'll easily graduate in June. Plus, structure helps me feel less like a wacko freak.

My library card rests beside the books. "Tiegen Richards, Regional Public Library, Woodsdale, Washington." I shove it deep in my jeans pocket, and straighten my grey sweatshirt. I'll study Monday through Thursday nights all summer. This is the first Monday since school ended. No better time to begin.

I sigh.

One man glances at me. I flash a brief-polite-smile, that dies before it reaches my eyes. I try for forgettable. He smiles back, but the other guy rants, pulling his attention away. They sure are on about something. *Bor-ing.* I crank my cellphone to concert volume.

Half an hour later, a librarian comes over. I have my tunes up so loud, he has to pass a hand in front of my face to get my attention. "Miss?"

I look up and pull out the earbuds, tangling one in my shoulder-length, light-brown hair. "Uh, sorry. Yeah?"

"Those men, does their volume bother you?"

I keep my eyes off of the men, now quiet, who must've heard. Instead, I shrug. "They're okay." I refocus on my book. *A low profile simplifies life.*

The librarian still asks the guys to lower their voices. They do, for ten minutes or so. That's when I realize, I left my earbuds out. *Great.*

"Next time, let's meet at the bar. What do you say?" the short one asks.

"Can't drink anymore. Lost my stupid wife to it. Gotta pay child support, so I can't afford to go out either. At least, it's free here. My only expense, since the divorce, is my health club membership."

He grinds his teeth, flexing huge jaw muscles. The corner of my eye studies the side of his face. Flex. Flex. Maybe he'll break a tooth.

2

He leans toward his buddy, whose greasy comb-over traverses a bald spot too humongous to hide. I expect a whisper, but no.

"How dare those guys at the club judge us? We're not terrorists in *their* country."

"You got that right." Baldy's chuckle is humorless.

"Our constitution gives them religious freedom. And *they* put *us* down?" Flexman's volume falls. "Someone should hand them a teaching." He taps a fist into his palm.

"Gonna play professor?" Baldy raises a brow.

"Could be," Flexman's chin juts forward.

"Oh yeah!" Baldy leans onto two back chair legs.

Their cruel words snag my thoughts. My concentration crumbles. *So much for studying.* I poke my buds in belatedly. With everything else that's going on in the world, I don't need more ugliness.

I gather up my things and, with conserved motion, slip out of my chair. Emanating invisibility, I turn toward the exit. I'm skilled at not being noticed.

Usually.

Before I walk two steps, Flexman jumps up. I sense him before I hear him. So I turn back, and paste on my polite may-I-help-you smile, before I realize that he is seething. He stares like there's a bullseye right between my eyes.

Flex. Flex. His nostrils flare.

Sweat seeps from my pores. My stomach lurches.

He strides forward and snatches my earbuds by their wires and flings them down. Pain zaps my ears, and my hands spring to cushion them.

He roars. "Why were you eavesdropping on us? I won't have it!"

The librarian comes up and tries to shush him, which is like trying to turn back a flood with a single sandbag, but I seize the chance to back around him. I turn and dart towards the door. Another bellow explodes behind me.

"I'll slap you black and blue—teach you not to listen to other people's conversations!"

My breath gasps as I race out the door towards my car.

"I'm calling 911!" The librarian calls out after us.

My earbuds plop against my right knee from the pocket of my jeans where they plug into my phone. My legs seem slow, and I strain to widen each pace.

On the run, I scrabble my key out of my left pocket and press the unlock button, way before I reach the car. I dive inside, lock the door behind me, start the motor, and put the car in reverse, before I dart a glance through the front windshield at my pursuer. Flexman is only a step from my bumper.

I swing my head around and gun the motor. Tires shriek as I arc the car around backwards. Flex runs up beside me, his open mouth drooling, his bulging eyes steely gray, and smacks the car's hood.

I see police running toward the library from the P.D., just down the block. Maybe they'll arrest the guy. My foot plunges the accelerator to the floor, the car leaps forward, and Flexman rolls away. The car scoots into the street, barely missing a silver Toyota coupe that brakes, blasting its horn.

When I look back from the corner, I no longer see my attacker, and I suck oxygen, trying to slow my heart. My face is wet. *I'm crying?* I give in and let tears streak my cheeks.

I drive erratically at first. As my mind clears, I fight for self-control, and slow down. The police must have him. *Breathe. Just get home safely for now.*

I pull into my garage, wipe my face, blow my nose, and then smile into the rearview mirror. I audition, "Hello," three or four times with various smiles. I press my fingers against the window glass, and touch the cool tips onto the reddened skin on my face. Hopefully, I look less like a ghoul now.

On the front porch, I take two slow, full breaths, stretch, and shake rigidity out of my upper back. My hair bounces around my shoulders. What I want most is to slip into the house unseen. If I talk much, I'll sob. It's over now, and there's no reason to worry my folks. Plus, I need time to re-cover alone. I turn the knob, smile, and push open the door.

My parents sit across from each other in the living room. They look up expectantly as I enter, and I'm shocked at how gray their hair has become. Why hadn't I noticed before?

"Hi." I give them only brief eye contact. I shoot them an excuse-me-I've-got-lots-to-do smile and beeline toward my room. The acting job of the year.

Dad's voice stops me. "What's your hurry, hon?"

"Did you work productively at the library? Will that work out okay?" Mom sets down a necklace she is beading.

"It was fine." I offer no details that they can weave into a conversation but start for my room again. I crave privacy. No matter how well I get along with Mom and Dad, I don't want to go into what happened yet. It's too raw. Maybe in the morning.

"Stay and talk with us awhile," Dad bookmarks what he had been reading, and sets it aside. "Finals kept you so busy the last couple of weeks that we've hardly spoken a word to each other." His voice stops me again. This time I must tell them something. Get them to sympathize.

"I feel the same, Dad. But tonight's not the night. I'm beat. Maybe tomorrow after you get home from work?" I give a hopeful smile—one he usually can't resist.

"Okay, sweetheart. I'll look forward to it." He slumps back into the couch. "Good-night."

I toss them each a kiss—a gesture we've shared all my life. They respond in kind, and I give a little wave before I vanish.

I deserve an Oscar.

I shower, brush my teeth and put on warm pajamas. Then, although it's still light outside, I climb into bed where I shake for an age or two, my eyes staring blindly while the library scene loops on eternal replay behind them.

Chapter 2

The moment I awaken in the morning, I grab my journal and scrawl down everything I recall from last night. My heart races. In a moment, I'm immersed in the drama again. My breath comes fast.

Then, I read through my brain dump and start to organize it.

Creating two columns: Real and Dream, I tweeze the details out with effort. Running back through yesterday in my mind, I discover a faint overlapping memory: of calmly leaving the library, driving home, and getting into bed as normal. At first, I wonder if the memory was from another day, since it's so similar to many trips home over the years.

I call the library, and ask the day librarian if the police were there last night. "The police," she says, "at the library?"

"I take it that's a no." I give my silly-me laugh.

"No, I don't believe so, dear. Do you want to check with them? I have their number."

"I'm fine. I just wondered what I saw, driving by. Nothing, it seems. Thanks." I hang up. Then I call the police department with the same question. No drama at the library yesterday.

Thinking through the possibilities, now that I've had a good night's sleep, I recognize that the attack at the library has a nightmarish quality that often indicates a dream. Nightmares are a gift in that way, though I didn't believe it as a kid.

Back then, before I had developed any ability to untangle dreams and reality, the certain knowledge of monsters, as real to me as my parents, dwelt with me 24/7. Other kids asked their parents for a nightlight to keep the monsters at bay when they're little. I knew better. Light didn't affect my monsters. I asked for a bazooka. Unfortunately, Dad thought I was kidding.

I note my two conflicting memories in different columns of my journal: leaving-the-library-as-usual vs. the-crazed-flight-home. I deduce that the attack didn't happen, and the calm version is my real memory. It's the harder to recall, because so little emotion is woven into ordinary repetitions. There's no reason to code it into long-term memory. Dreams often lack the ordinariness of real life.

"The attack was a dream," I murmur to myself. Repeating it aloud helps the truth take precedence in my screwed-up brain. During the flashbacks I expect to experience today, I'll repeat it numerous times.

Remembering the attack, dream or not, still makes me tremble, because, unfortunately, I dream in Blue Ray. And unlike normal people, my dreams don't fade as I awaken. I have learned that in real life, my eye-witness experiences may never have happened. My journal is my most potent determiner of the truth.

The library is still a safe place for my studies, regardless of how I feel this moment. *The library is safe. The library is safe. The library is safe.* I make an effort to code that into memory as well.

My shoulders release. I hunch and relax them several times and add a couple of shoulder rolls, too. The attack was a dream. It had to be.

I journal on, teasing out the other handful of dreams from amongst yesterday's experiences. I chew my lower lip, determined to stay in control of my dream material. I will not allow it to seep into my day. *Take control of your life.*

This is my daily routine. I've become good at it.

I've seen a psychiatrist about the dream thing. Dr. Crenshaw found no evidence in the psych literature that others live with this particular dream disorder. People who suffer psychotic breaks may mix dreams into real life. But those with severe illnesses have little insight into what is reality vs. fiction. They can't sort out events like I can. Which means I'm sane, in my unique, crazy way. The dreams are more of a disability.

What's scary is, the doc admitted a few years back, that my dreams might presage mental illness. She was especially concerned about Schizophrenia since I was 20, when it often manifests. So I concentrate on keeping my two worlds separate. If I can keep from ending up a nutcase, I'll do it. I have other plans for my life.

After I re-read yesterday's journal posts and check my calendar, I believe I've caged the dream world away for another day. Though I'm overly vigilant at first, I hum along with Spotify, and throw in a few dance steps as I make my breakfast. The awkwardness eases.

I smirk at the mirror me, and try not to envy her controlled world. *I've got this.*

Score one for the real me.

9

* * *

Later, I drop by the mall to pick out new athletic shoes. Rounding a corner, I brush up against my ex-boyfriend from last summer, Chase. He's with two of his friends. I don't see who they are at first. I turn to apologize and hear Chase say, "That one's mental." He circles a finger at the side of his head and nods toward me. His friends snicker.

My stomach does a flip, and I turn away. *Ouch!* And here I was going to apologize for bumping into him. *Did I really date this ox?* I need to seriously reevaluate my taste in men.

Last summer Chase mentioned a stock he thought I should invest in. I earned so little interest from my savings account that a mouse would have starved. So, I researched the stock and decided it'd be a good investment—not high yield, but safe. In fact, I bought a fair-sized chunk.

It bottomed out on me. I lost my entire investment.

When I rechecked online, I realized that I'd never gone there before. I'd only dreamt that I investigated the stock. One glance told me that, had I examined it, even once, I wouldn't have invested.

My dreams get me into trouble. They certainly won that round.

Mom and Dad understood about it, though. They wanted to help. So they are letting me live at home, rent free, until I finish my doctorate. If I graduate next year, this may be my last summer with them. That's important, too. Family.

The folks lent me their second car. A third car would cost too much—just for maintenance and gas. I like to say that I'm reducing greenhouse emissions, a cause I truly support. I also prefer it to admitting that I'm in debt. Deep debt.

My VISA card is maxed.

While I reestablish my equilibrium, I sit by a fountain and flip through the contacts stored in my cell phone, wanting to talk to someone. There's nobody who would understand what just happened with my ex. My circle of friends is small, primarily other grad students. Most are traveling this summer, and I don't want to ruin that. I slip the phone back into my pocket. I feel a little better, though, just reading their names.

Glancing up, I see this guy I sort of know, James, who lives a few blocks from me. He stands even in height, about five eleven, next to a stranger wearing a vintage woven cap like I've seen at the theater. Brown hair curls at its edge. I change directions and check out the newcomer more closely. He's nicely built, but not muscle-bound that I can tell. He has a pleasant face, brown eyes framed by long lashes, and just a touch of beard shadowing his oval face. He smiles.

"Hey James, how are things?" I blurt. I don't pass him by, like usual, with nice-to-see-you pasted on my face so he'll immediately forget me.

"Oh, hi, Tieg. I'm good. Uh, this is Geoffrey, from England. His parents and mine have been friends for -- maybe forever. He's spending the summer at my place before he starts UDub this fall for a master's in education."

"Hey." Geoffrey doffs his cap and bows. "Geoff, if you please." His crushed waves bounce out around his face as his milk chocolate eyes sparkle.

His voice makes my mouth water, even though his gesture was a bit dramatic. Between his accent and his odd hat, I'm intrigued. I open my mouth, but if anything comes out, it's so soft even I can't hear it. He looks at me, passing his cap from hand to hand as he waits, and his smile seems genuine, if a touch anxious. I clear my throat and try again.

"That's where I'm going, too." Then on impulse, I stick out my hand like some corporate nerd.

He shakes it formally, as if everyone does stuff like that. "A pleasure." How formal!

11

James speaks up. "Tiegen's folks live a few streets over. We've been neighbors since middle school."

It's nice of him. James is someone I don't hang with anymore, though we used to run with the same group of friends. We drifted apart after high school. Across the way from us, a twenty-something woman in a casual pantsuit, carrying a baby, catches my eye. The kid holds a multi-colored teething ring, out over her mother's shoulder, and drops it to the ground. The baby stares at it on the ground, then fusses while her mom walks on, oblivious. "Oops. Just a sec." I fly over to retrieve the toy. The mother thanks me and the toddler gazes at me, wide-eyed, with most of one hand crammed in her mouth.

I jog back, laughing at the munchkin. "Sorry to interrupt. That mom looked like she could use a hand. Her little girl is adorable."

"No worries — it's cool," Geoff says. "Kids are ace. In fact, my major is Special Ed. This is the first summer in eons that I won't be a camp counselor. Had to choose between that and crossing the pond."

"At a camp for kids with disabilities," James says.

"Yeah." Geoff nods. "Many never went to camp before. I'll miss watching their self-confidence grow during the week in the woods."

"I get along great with kids." I don't add that they usually like me, unlike adults who, once they hear about my dreams, condescend to me.

"Before I ran off, I was about to say that I attend University of Washington — Udub — too. This summer I'm gaining a head start on readings for my doctoral dissertation in political science. It's on human rights." Better. I said something halfway normal without tripping over my tongue.

"Lovely!" Geoff squeezes his hands together. "Let's get together this summer and you can give me a heads-up about the U." He dons his cap with a flair of his wrist, somehow taming most of the curls, and gives a tiny chuckle. His eyes flick away then, self-consciously, I imagine. But that just attracts me. He seems authentic.

Assuming my laryngitis has passed, summer just got more intriguing.

* * *

Wednesday morning, I tidy up the dishes, tie on my new lavender Skechers, and emerge into a typically gorgeous summer morning in the Pacific NW, the most beautiful place on Earth. True, we get tons of rain, but that creates a luscious green summertime, while the nearby Puget Sound keeps the heat down. Air quality is usually good as well, unlike in larger cities. I fill my lungs and exhale delight.

On impulse, I stride towards the street where James lives. To my delight, Geoff waves at me through the window, then pops out the front door.

He whips off his cap, and says, "It's Tiegen, right? Are you on a special mission, or may I walk with you?"

He looks so hopeful in his Dickens hat that I'm reminded of Oliver Twist, asking for more food at the orphanage. I smile. How can I turn down such a winsome character? And his accent, well...

"Yeah, come."

"Righto. I'm keen for a morning ramble. Back at home, on the usual weekend, my da and I walk the fields or scramble the *ghylls*."

"Ghyll scrambling?"

"Climbing ravines. I live in Cumbria – the lake district – where these water-twisted places call out to explorers. At least they have to us over the years."

"Cool. I geocache our ravines. But no ghylls today. Let's head toward the coast. You'll get a glimpse of Puget Sound and the Olympic Mountains before we turn back."

"Brilliant." He falls into step beside me, bouncing a bit. "So Tiegen. What are your plans this summer?" He struggles a bit at starting the conversation. I glance at him, and his mouth looks tight.

"I hope to get a job—make some money. I have an interview set up Thursday morning for a research assistant position in a human rights study."

"That could help with your dissertation."

"That's the plan. What about you?"

He shrugs. "I'm on holiday here. My parents and James' set it up. I may travel as well. But as a master's student, I don't have to study this summer."

"Lucky."

He nods. "I am, that." He seemed more relaxed until he ran out of words. Now he's pressing his lips together.

We walk in silence for a bit, and the warm sunshine is a heavenly contrast to last night's nightmare. A breeze blows my hair back, cooling my throat.

"What's your hometown? Somewhere rural?"

"Well, Keswick is smallish, but green like here. We have festivals, mountains, and history all around us. My da and I live near the edge of town. He's a barrister, a traditional Englishman." He poses as stately for a moment, his face noble. Then he shoots me a quick look. "Not outhouses and wooden stoves, mind you. We're not that out of touch." He flicks a hand near his head and makes a face. "But traditional education, outdoorsy activities, honesty, and what I suppose one'd call chivalry. He's big on developing one's character."

That fits with his cap and roaming the fields with his father. Listening to his accent, I can almost imagine taking a step back in time with him.

"The library's been strange lately." I tell him what Flexman and Baldy said. "Then I had a nightmare about Flexman chasing me out of the library, yelling. I guess they made a bigger impression on me than I realized." I toss off a little laugh to downplay the nightmare's importance. Then I give him a friendly smile.

"I hope you got back to sleep, after. Anxiety dreams—" He pulls his mouth sideways, his face finishing the sentence.

"So, you like the library?"

"I've loved it there since I was a kid. If I study there four nights a week, I can plow through my reading and note-taking this summer."

"My Mum was a librarian. She didn't think of it as work. She felt spoiled taking a salary for something she enjoyed so much."

"That interview I have in a couple of days?" I say. "That work could feel similar. At least, I've imagined it that way. I might become a human rights activist."

"I want to teach special education awhile, then sit for my Ph.D. and become a university professor," Geoff says. "I plan to help people with disabilities. But as you say, it may not be all I hoped once I get there."

"That'll be a huge shift. You'll do research at a university, if you want a tenured position, right?

"Yeah. I have done already—training physically-disabled kids to become self-sufficient—for the past two years. Started as an undergrad. One reason I applied to UW is because the master's department there does similar research.

"My advisor suggested several institutions for furthering my work. This one is physically closest to James' family, and has a respected program. The website called it 'one of the Public Ivies,' which Da really liked."

"Bet you'll be glad. There are kids in every country like those at your camp. You could help children wherever you settle."

"I'd like to contribute. Research is teamwork, though. Nobody makes great breakthroughs alone."

"I suppose you're right. The same will probably be true of me."

We reach an overlook where a break in the trees allows us to see distant boats on the water. Even though much of the winter snow is gone, the Olympic Mountains show brush strokes of white at their peaks — glaciers that will last the year through. We lean against the railing and enjoy the view for a few minutes before we start back. A salty breeze blows against our faces.

"Hey, tell me — do you have pubs about? I've not seen any," Geoff asks.

"Pubs? A few copies, but it's not an American thing. We have great micro-breweries, though, if you crave beer. Or are you looking for food?"

"Entertainment mostly -- a place to gather with locals over a pint."

"A brewery then."

"Coming here, I missed the annual Keswick Beer Festival." His glance seems to check how I take that. "It's always a favorite of mine. Maybe we could take in a brewery and raise a pint to home?" He offers an air-toast, lifts his eyebrows and tilts his head.

My heart does a cartwheel in my chest. *He's asking me out.*

"I'd love to, but tonight I have plans. How about this weekend?"

"Excellent. Plan on it." He gives me a little wink.

We are back on my street now, heading toward home. "Shall we walk tomorrow morning?" Geoff asks, and I nod. "I'll give you my number. About the same time?"

I glow, and we program each other's numbers into our cells. "Cool. See you then."

He doffs his cap for a wave good-bye and continues down the street, with a bouncing gait. Maybe he feels as happy as I do. I hope so.

* * *

Tonight I leave early for the library. I want a quiet seat with space for my books. What a gift it would be if my dreams faded away like normal people's. Then my nerves about finding a seat might not seem so important.

But inside the library, almost every seat is either already claimed or sits beside a stranger. Except, of course, a small empty table next to the men from yesterday. Two nights in a row? With my dream memories clearer in my head than last night's reality, I can't help but want to keep my distance, rational or not. I stand still, thinking.

I decide to find a fiction book to check out—a summer read to rest my brain from the academic grind. Maybe, in the meantime, a spot will open up at another table.

I want something as opposite as I can imagine from my scholarly reading—something escapist. I find a detective novel about a zombie killing. The author appears to take the concept seriously. The walking dead should scare you stupid. I don't like cutesy zombie stuff. Not at all.

When I journey back from the stacks, the library is more crowded than before. No new spots have opened up. In fact, several are gone.

My feet drag as I return to last night's table. *The library is safe. The library is safe.* But the guys talk more softly tonight. I'm pretty sure my music will block them out.

After a few minutes, my brain's study center takes over, and the homey stacks vanish. In one book, I find a quote about an issue I want to elucidate in my introduction. Bingo. A bibliography addition. When I eventually pack up for the night, my success excites me. This is the type of work I planned to tackle. And it's going quicker than I'd hoped.

I remove my buds and tuck away my phone. Suddenly, I hear Flexman's voice.

"You bet. It's about time I show them what's what. First, I'll follow each one home from the gym and find out where he lives. Then, bam!" He claps his hands on the last word, and cackles.

Startled, my elbow bumps my library card and some notes I'd taken onto the floor between me and the two men. I bend over, shuffle them together and scoop them up.

Carefully, I avoid eye contact, remembering my dream. Whether or not these guys are capable of violence, I'm going to take the possibility seriously. I stuff the notes into the front pocket of my pack, and then slink off to the door, trying to hide in another dimension. I want to leave unnoticed — even more so than usual.

The public library, my sanctuary since childhood, seems filled with shadows. I can't wait to get away.

* * *

When Geoff knocks in the morning, I'm reading my detective novel. I let him in. As he passes me, I smell marijuana smoke. I pull back instinctively.

"What's the matter?"

"I-I didn't know you smoked."

"Just a spot of green to soothe the nerves. I gave up cigs over a year ago. Cannabis's legal here, right?"

18

I nod, suddenly feeling like a prude. I'm probably the only twenty-something in Washington who hasn't tried grass, though for good reason. I let the subject drop.

"You're reading this?" He picks up my book. "Detective novels are my favorite read."

"Me too. And this one has a zombie in it as well. It should be exciting."

"Let me know what you think. I might read it too." We step outside and I lock the door.

During our walk I tell him about last night's conversation between Flexman and Baldy. He listens, serious, hands in his pants pockets. Then he meets my eyes and stops.

"You think they mean to hurt someone then?" He rolls forward and back on his feet a couple of times, hands stuffed in his pockets.

"How could I know? But my stomach hurts when I consider it. So maybe."

"What can you do about it?"

"Not much. I don't know the guys' names or where they live."

"Maybe the coppers have run into them before."

"May-be," I say again, stretching out the word. I don't like this turn of conversation, though what did I expect? That Geoff suggest I forget about the library guys? Like I can't do that for myself. Now who's acting like an adult?

"At the library tonight, I could come along and check out those blokes." Geoff throws a couple of Popeye punches at the air. "If you want the company." The stroke of flirtation in his look makes my knees go wobbly. His accent melts me like ice in hot tea.

"Oh, definitely." I dart a similar look back to him before I go on. "Chances are, they won't come. But if they are there, I could sit at my usual table with my earbuds in, but off. You could hide in the stacks—maybe snap pictures when it's safe. If I decide to talk to the police later, I might use them."

"Will do. Even without the fisticuffs. What time?" Geoff squeezes his hands together. I wonder whether it's excitement or nerves.

As we work out the details, my stomach pangs a couple times. It doesn't matter, though. My stomach and I have had to coexist for a long time.

We walk quietly then, each thinking separate thoughts. When we get to my house, I say, "So, see you tonight?"

"No problem. I'll be here." He tucks a wisp of hair behind my ear. "Ta." He brushes my shoulder with his hand before he turns away.

My laryngitis is back with a bang, and I feel my face flush. Thankfully he doesn't look back. I watch his figure recede.

You know, looking at him now, he seems more like Scrooge's handsome nephew, Fred, than like Oliver Twist. I can't stop beaming.

Chapter 3

The rest of the afternoon drags as I work on the readings from my advisor. If I don't plan to work in the library tonight, I need to do it now. It should be fun having Geoff along, especially if the weird guys don't show.

Finally, after I inhale a quick dinner, Geoff raps on the door.

We go in my car but enter the library about ten minutes apart. The guys are there again.

I park myself at the same open table, and pile my resources in front of me as usual. This time, I listen, earbuds in but music off, for any sign of threat. From time to time, I turn a page or jot a note so I look authentic. Their voices are soft, and I imagine my right ear turning to their words like a flower to sunlight.

Geoff wanders the stacks with his cellphone. Now and then I glimpse him, always in a different place. When our eyes meet, Geoff crinkles his nose or flutters his eyes at me. Once he winks. I struggle not to laugh. He's mainly taking pics of me. My eyes seek where he'll pop up next, though surreptitiously. The game distracts me. Good thing I only pretend to study.

When I check out the men from the corner of my eye, I see no change in their behavior. They don't notice Geoff, which is perfect.

Their conversation grumbles — mostly about their homes, their pay — general dissatisfaction with life, it seems. Even figuring in dream complications, my existence is a celebration compared to theirs. I feel sorry for them, wondering how life managed to wear them down so thoroughly. My mind drifts as I catch sight of Geoff again, his cap pulled low over his eyes.

"Why'd the athletic facility let in that scum?" Flexman says. "It's up-scale otherwise. Those infidels should find their own place."

My ears return to receiver mode.

"Things have gone downhill, that's for sure," Baldy shakes his head. "Time was, when you hardly saw an immigrant. They stayed in their own neighborhoods where we didn't see them. The system worked. Now, even illegals want good wages and a medical plan. I know who ends up paying for that." He taps his chest, raising his chin, and bulging out his lower lip. "So we end up meeting at the library instead of over a steak."

Flexman nods like a sage. "We're of a mind on that subject, my friend."

Baldy grunts, nodding concurrence.

"Hey, I meant to tell you — I've been thinking about them."

"So. You have a plan?" Baldy sounds excited.

Flexman leans in and lowers his voice. I keep my body still, but my ears blossom wider still.

"They've got to get it -- that they're not welcome -- so I'll hit them in two stages. First time, I'll humble them a little. Something odd that nobody expects in quiet, old Woodsdale. Then, I'll stun them with a major hurting — take them down hard. Maybe both together, if I can work it out."

"Wish I could watch their faces. That would be better than a Monster Truck crash-down."

I continue to listen, but little else seems relevant. I've heard plenty. More than I want to know. A perilous amount. Flexman's face, red and quivering, screams at me from my dream scene. I'm asking for it — eavesdropping for real.

I pick my stuff up and stash it in my pack. Then I move toward the exit — one autumn leaf among many blowing by. Nothing to notice.

Geoff will meet me outside in a few.

* * *

My chest lightens when Geoff climbs into my car. After I left, I worried that the men might go after him, though logically, it seemed very unlikely. I can't stop grinning at him now, since he's in one piece.

"Tiegen, you okay? You left rather suddenly."

Happiness washes over me knowing that Geoff worried about me as well. He seems more substantial now than he did in the library, his good-humored face touched with concern, even twitching a little bit. I fill him in on the conversation during our drive home, describing how I imagined Flexman coming after me for eavesdropping.

He whistles and twists toward me on the seat. "Maybe you need some distance from them." He rests an arm on my shoulder, and rubs the back of my neck.

The pressure pulls an appreciative "Mmm" out of me.

"I must admit, I'm not as comfortable at the library as I used to be." I sigh. "At least I can take a break for the weekend."

I no longer smell smoke on Geoff's clothes. He must have showered in addition to changing clothes before coming out tonight.

"So, what next?" he asks.

"Not sure. If these weren't middle-aged, white men, I know their threats would be taken seriously. Racism may be subtler than it used to be, but it's still strong in the dominant population, and these guys benefit." I scowl, thinking.

"You know my job interview tomorrow? It was rescheduled to Monday morning. I can use that time if I decide to visit the police department. They must be trained to deal with situations like this."

"Good thinking. I'll send you a few piccies just in case."

He doesn't push, which I appreciate, as the whole idea makes my gut squirm. In fact, he changes the topic.

"So, is it the brewery tomorrow night? It'll be Friday."

I pull the car into the driveway and hit the remote. The garage door rises in its noisy, dependable way.

"Yeah. May as well enjoy the summer." I don't even try to put on my sweetest smile for him—it's already there.

"Ace." He beams.

"You don't want to spend the time with James?"

"When I can be with you? What do you think?" He raises his eyebrows. "He has his own schedule." He pronounces it "shedule," which is cool.

We sit there for a moment, grinning idiotically at each other. I struggle for words that won't sound stupid. I glance down at my lap, and when I look back up, his face is very close to mine. He kisses me softly on the cheek and gives me a lingering look.

I have a floaty feeling inside. He caught me off guard. That silly smile stretches my mouth wide. "Well, thanks for the help tonight." Immediately I berate myself mentally for chilling the moment.

But Geoff's eyes sparkle. "Any time, blue eyes." He hops out of the car, gives a wave, and runs toward James' house, like energy bursts out of him.

But pulling the car into the garage, my joy fades. How long do I expect Geoff to think I'm worth dating? I remember my ex, Chase, and his comment to his friends. He never wanted to understand about my dreams; he just wanted me "fixed." When I wasn't, he labeled me a nut case and broke up with me. I hid in my room for a week, but I couldn't blame Chase for thinking I was mental.

Sometimes I think the same.

Chapter 4

After waking up and writing in my dream journal, and before I can talk myself out of it, I zip over to the police station in my car. I walk inside and look around, out of place, my stomach already regretting the trip.

"May I help you?" A man at the front desk stands up.

"I don't know." To my ears, I sound exceptionally stupid. "Um, what I mean is—" I breathe deeply. "I overheard a couple of guys griping at the library. One of them had a plan to hurt a couple of people."

"Let me call an officer in to take your statement, miss." He picks up a phone. "Officer St. Marie? A young woman at the front desk would like to report a possible impending crime." He hangs up. "She'll be right out."

I swallow hard. It was difficult enough to speak up at the front desk. Now I have to start over again. And for an official statement, too. I'm glad I didn't over-think this visit earlier—I might never have made it here.

The police woman comes to the desk and extends her hand.

"Tiegen Richards."

I nod and swallow.

"My office is down the hall. We can talk there."

I follow behind her, relieved, curiously, by her athletic appearance. She doesn't seem much older than me. Maybe twenty-seven—twenty-eight. Not as intimidating as I feared. It helps that she's a woman.

Her office is a cubicle in a suite with high walls. The nameplate reads: "Officer Jessica Saint Marie." It's a good name. My shoulders sag. I'm just a concerned citizen—doing what any responsible person would do. Right?

I recap what I overheard and my suspicions about Flexman and Baldy. Seeing there are open spaces beneath the walls, I speak softly, hoping my voice won't carry.

"You don't know the name or address of those planning the attack or of the potential victims, correct?" She keyboards my responses into her laptop.

"Only that the schemers meet at the Woodsdale Public Library in the evening. At least, I've seen them there each night this week so far, while I worked on my dissertation."

"All right—that's fine. The incident is active in our files. If a crime occurs fitting this description, may I call you so we can talk again?"

Wait. She's not going to the library herself?

"I guess so. But honestly, that's all I know. I hoped you'd stop anything bad from happening." Clearly, I don't know squat, and I'm about as likely to hear from her as I am to drop through a manhole cover into the jaws of aliens. My description was as vague as the statements I overheard. Police may occasionally act on hunches, but not on this one. Mine was a wasted visit, even if a real crime is being planned.

27

"Your phone number?"

I rattle it off.

"Is that your cell phone?"

"Yeah. The landline where I live is—" I rattle that off, too, before I realize she never asked for it. *Now I'm jabbering. Great.* "Meanwhile, if you hear more, let me know. Unless they act on their threats, there isn't much I can do. But in case they do, I appreciate having this lead to follow up. Thank you, Tiegen."

She stands up and offers me her hand again. I shake it and turn to the door, eager to escape. *I'm superfluous here.*

As I close the main door behind me, I wonder if I'd have bothered to come in, if not for the talk with Geoff. He made the risk of violence seem plausible. Or was I the one who did that? Anyway, it's over and I've done my good citizen thingy. It's police business now, no longer mine. I can forget it.

I hope.

* * *

Towards evening, I grow more and more excited about the brewery with Geoff. Tonight has a different feel—like our relationship is more official somehow. A real date.

I take extra time to pick out my best casual outfit including a lowcut aqua top. A silver necklace and simple earrings go well with it and my black pants. Then I touch up my makeup so it is just right and brush my hair into fluffiness. A dab of my favorite scent tops off my efforts. I squint at the mirror. I look a lot more confident—even a bit like Officer St. Marie.

Not bad.

I take off in the car to pick Geoff up at his place. I don't even have to get out before he's coming down his front walkway towards me, walking so quickly that he's almost running.

"Hey Tiegen." He slides into the seat beside me, without his cap for the first time. He looks delicious, and I'm relieved that I properly gauged the importance of this first date. I don't smell cannabis on him, but I can see by his pupils that he needed some to calm his nerves.

"Hey Geoff. You look great."

He blushes, then rubs his knuckles against one cheek and examines them as if checking whether great brushes off. He looks down at his lap, as if for inspiration, then back at me. "So which brewery are we off to?"

"Sound Brews moved into what used to be an old warehouse near the water. It must have been something special during the logging boom. The original timbers still show in the ceiling, though the rest is modern.

"You'll see the sunset if you face the water. Or we can sit at the bar. I love their happy hour snacks. We'll find out what's on tap tonight before we order. I haven't been there recently enough to know. Sound okay?"

"Lovely. But I doubt the sunset will look better than you."

Now it's my turn to blush. "Thanks."

* * *

Sound Brews is crowded, and we end up sitting with others at a largish table. That seems to fit Geoff's expectations, and he visits with those near us, who are fascinated by a Brit in their local bar. He seems right at home.

I am quiet, but enjoy watching Geoff in his element. He tries three different beers while I nurse one.

"I read this Internet joke." He gestures with his half-empty mug. "Let's see if I remember it. 'A Muslim, a Jew, a

29

Hindu, a Christian and an atheist enter a bar and sit together. You know what happens?'"

If anyone knows the punchline, they don't ruin his moment by telling it. They laugh and shake their heads no and ask, "What?"

"They drink some pints and have a wonderful evening together — because they're not a bunch of shiteheads!'"

I laugh with the group at the unexpected ending. Someone says, "Sounds like real life." Everyone laughs again.

By the time we leave, Geoff's all bouncy again. "That was fantastic."

"For me, too. Was it as good as a pub?"

"Even better, considering the company." He winks at me.

I make sure he sees the happiness in my face.

He gives me a long kiss before he slides out at his house.

The kiss makes my toes curl.

* * *

Geoff calls in the morning as I finish breakfast.

"Last night was lovely. Thanks again," he says.

"Any time. Want to geocache? It's my hobby."

"Sure. Would it fit with a bike ride?James drives everywhere, so he offered me his bicycle for the summer."

Geoff sounds inordinately pleased when I say yes. Like everything having to do with Geoff, it's a bit strange. But biking's a good way to save money on gas.

I invite him over. We make sandwiches while chatting about the brewery adventure, and then stack them into my backpack. I add two water bottles filled with home-brewed sun tea and a bag of golden Rainier cherries for dessert.

I thrust my arms through the straps and hand him a rolled up blanket in case the picnic tables are full.

We glide over to Wilcox Park, and then wander up into the tree-covered hills. I show him a geocache I've hidden nearby. At first, he doesn't see it. Then I pick it up and set it into his hand.

"I don't know what it is." He examines the slender container.

"It's a game. You look up the GPS coordinates of a geocache online, and then you hunt for it. You sign your name on the log inside, and add it to your count on the website." I open the container, pull out a miniscule roll of paper, and show him the signatures. My handle's at the top.

"Geomojo? That's you?"

"Yeah. I liked the sound of it. You can choose any name. Then you hide the cache exactly the same way for the next geocacher. It sounds strange, but it's easy to get addicted to the feeling of triumph when you make the find."

He laughs, then reaches into his pocket. "When I first saw it, I thought you were pulling out one of these." In his hand is a blunt and a lighter. "Want a hit? I had a little before I came over. It's good stuff—very mellow."

"No thanks. I only use alcohol, and not much of that." My hands go clammy, and I look away from the hand-rolled drug. It's another potential deal breaker in this relationship.

"No worries." He slips both joint and lighter back in his pocket. "It calms me down, but a drink can do that too."

I re-hide the geocache and decide I'll stick to my make-no-waves resolution for now. Let's just enjoy this afternoon together.

But I wonder how often he gets high.

* * *

Geoff and I ride out along the Interurban Trail and search for geocaches. The breeze in my face feels wonderful. My hands grow moist on the handlebars, and I know the sun will bake us toasty warm once we stop.

I check my GPS app, and we pull over in a beautiful spot. Three tall pines guard a shady niche where the cache should be. Last time, I came up with the container, but Geoff finds this one.

"I'll be Cagycacher." He signs the log. Our fingers brush as he hands it to me. Then he slips the geocache back into hiding.

"You are stellar at this." He brushes dirt off his fingers. "But I'm glad I found this one."

"You're doing fine. It gets easier with practice, like anything. You'll probably find most of them one of these days — leave me in the dust."

"Never!" He laughs. "You are right about the addiction factor. Now that I've found one, I can't wait to grab the next one."

"Just wait. It gets stronger the more you find."

We climb back on our bikes and cruise down the pathway. Parts of the Interurban run along the road, or next to overgrown blackberry bushes, while other parts border parks. I see things I never noticed before I had Geoff along — graceful branches, wildflowers. I view it through two pairs of eyes, one dewdrop fresh.

Blackberry canes grow everywhere, but their fruit won't ripen for a month or two. As invasive as they are, their flavor floods sweetly into memory. I swallow.

"Help me pick those once they get ripe, and I'll bake a pie for you," I call out to Geoff, pointing as he whizzes along beside me.

"Will do."

I stop so we can pick salmonberries when their namesake color flashes amid the green vines. We eat these raw, some bland, some tart, feeding each other the juiciest ones. Geoff wipes the juice from my lips.

My mouth must look like the Cheshire Cat's.

* * *

During lunch I decide to share more about my disability. A little more, anyway.

"So, about my dreams, they've always been vivid and unfading, except for the vague bits with little logic to them. I don't pay much attention to those."

I watch his face closely, afraid his openness will close down, but it doesn't. So I explain some tricks I use to figure out whether a memory is real or not.

I don't tell him I've been hospitalized twice on the nutty-ninth floor, though. Some things are too much for most people to handle.

I don't want to sound too wacko, but I want to be authentic. Or am I just pushing him a little so he leaves me now instead of at a more painful later? Remembering Chase, I choose my words carefully. But he seems fine, and I breathe away some tension.

"I guess Flexman and Baldy didn't terrorize anyone last night," I say. "If nothing happens by Sunday night, it was probably smack talk."

"You sound disappointed. But that's good, right — that nobody's hurt?"

"Of course. Only Jessica St. Marie may believe I made up the story. Part of me wants to prove that my word is reliable, even if it means a hate crime has to be committed. Lame, huh?"

"Not so. It's just that you don't deal with coppers every day." He shrugs.

* * *

Later that afternoon, in a grassy pocket park, we sit back under a tree.

"What's this one's name?" He points at its trunk.

33

"A madrona. See its thick green leaves and ruddy bark? It's unique. Like a transplant from another planet, I think."

"Hey brill, Tiegen." He gets that right away. So fun.

Parents and kids play nearby, but they ignore us. Geoff and I hold hands, and when I meet his eyes he kisses my mouth. I kiss back, wanting more. Despite the smell of smoke on his clothes, he doesn't taste of it. In fact, he tastes delicious.

A boy about eight years old chases a Frisbee in our direction and comments, "Eww. Gross!" So we pull apart and Geoff smirks at me and then nods toward our bikes. We get up and brush the grass from our clothes. Then Geoff waves to the little boy, gives me one more kiss before the boy can look away, and we ride off, laughing.

My heart rushes as the world streaks by. With the speed, a weightlessness overtakes me. I glance over at Geoff, imagining that our wheels may lift from the ground at any moment. "Wheeeeeeee!" I call out.

We fly together along the trail.

Chapter 5

When I slip out of bed Monday morning after journaling, I pull up the police crime blotter on my phone. Let me see what unusual crimes happened over the weekend. A drunk driver ran into a mailbox, and somebody stole a car, took it on a joyride out of town, trashed it, and abandoned it. Hmmm.

Anything else? Several cases of identity theft. Shoplifting by an unnamed minor. A domestic dispute. Nothing sounds like Flexman and Baldy's hate crime.

My breathing slowed. Yet disappointment still lingered inside. Jessica St. Marie didn't exist for me until last week. Yet she's competent, beautiful and smart—just how I'd like to be. Just like the me in the mirror. *You will be what you make of yourself,* I advise myself using one of my many affirmations.

I roll my shoulders, and then take a deep breath. How can I expect my words to carry weight with others when I second-guess myself? I gaze in the mirror imagining a me-version of the officer. Loose-shouldered. Confident. Ready to make the world better for everyone.

Not bad.

I turn away, lift my chin, and prepare for my day. I have my interview for the research internship this morning.

* * *

Commuters fill the lanes on the drive to Bothell. Sometimes the Interstates are a fast way to get around, but during rush hour they just can't hold all the vehicles. I-405 moves as slowly as a surface street — worse I think, since the state turned its HOV lane into a toll lane. But I've planned ahead for lots of time to get to my appointment. An opportunity so perfect isn't likely to occur again, and I want to impress.

* * *

When I arrive, I can't tell where to go. Glimpsing no directional sign, I get out and look for other applicants waiting for the group interview. Somehow, I appear to be the only one. I glance at my cell to make sure I'm not late, but I'm about five minutes early. So I approach a woman at what may pass for a receptionist's desk.

"I'm Tiegen Richards, here for my interview for the internship. Where should I go?"

The woman blinks a couple of times, and then squints at me. "We don't have interviews on Mondays. Your name again?" She puts on reading glasses that hang from beads around her neck, takes a couple pages of paper from a low shelf next to a computer, and studies them with a scowl as if the glasses are a new inconvenience for her.

"Tiegen Richards." My voice is softer this time. I'm haunted by the sense that I've screwed up. But how could that be after all the care I took?

She looks over the top of her glasses at me. "Ms. Richards, I'm afraid your interview was scheduled for last Friday."

Crap. It's happened again.

Chapter 6

"I'm not sure how you misunderstood when the interview was scheduled. After we discussed it on the phone, I sent you a confirmation letter reiterating the date and time. Did you receive it?"

I pull the letter out of my pocket and hand it to her. "Yes. It's right here. But I got a call on Thursday asking if I could come Monday instead. That's why I didn't turn up on Friday. But I could have come—I was free." I bite my tongue to shut myself up.

My mind races as my stomach bubbles with acid. The call was real, wasn't it? I try to recall what happened just before and after it. Sometimes that helps.

"We rescheduled no appointments." Her voice is terse. "I'm Dr. Bakker and I would have called you had any change been made."

I begin to tremble, so I squish my hands into fists to freeze the tremor. "Perhaps I dreamed it." It sounds stupid, though I fear it's true. "I'm so sorry I missed the interview,

Dr. Bakker. I was really looking forward to hearing more about the position."

Tears push under my eyelids as my body takes up arms against me. I draw a deep breath, hoping it'll stop them from leaking out.

The woman peers at me for a moment. I must look as devastated as I feel. She comes to a decision.

"Well, no harm done. We all make an occasional mistake. I set up a second group interview at the same time on Thursday morning if you can come in then."

I barely hold back from throwing myself at her feet and hugging her ankles. "Yes, of course. I appreciate the second chance. I'll be there for certain."

"You do that. I'll send a new confirmation letter so you'll have the date in writing. Don't miss it next time."

"Oh, no. I won't. Thank you, Dr. Bakker. Thank you very much."

"You're welcome. I'll see you then."

She looks back down at her work, and I flee. My breath comes fast, and only with enormous effort do I keep from bursting into tears the moment I climb behind the wheel.

Why do these things happen to me?

* * *

I'm home earlier than I would have been sans the fiasco. Grabbing my journal, I look through it for clues about the changed interview date. I figure the call came Wednesday afternoon, but it might have been Tuesday. I can't be certain. I didn't write about the date change anywhere. That's how sure I was that the call was a fact. It held none of the nightmare quality my dreams often contain.

Fragment-dreams are the ones that trip me up the most. They are so brief that they provide few hints as to their falsity. Just like bits of my day.

I want to break something. But I grab my pillow and run into the bathroom instead. I push down on the flush handle, and then scream as loud as I can into the thick whiteness. Cycling water and goose down contain the sound. When my personal drama passes, I return to my room and do what I'm supposed to do when upset—mindfulness meditation.

Afterward, my rage has soured to disappointment. My stomach settles into armed truce—probably the best I can hope for, but just not enough. *What a major screw-up.* I continue breathing deeply as the tension begins to recur. I get a little dizzy.

Eventually, my thoughts stray to Geoff. I encourage them, playing with my memories of our times together—of his kisses. I indulge a fantasy that continues on from that point. My mood improves.

My pocket vibrates and I jump back to the present. As if he can hear my thoughts, it's Geoff.

"I've been thinking of you, Tiegen -- how was the interview?"

"Um, not great. Can we talk in person?" I'm wary of my earlier excess of anger. I also need to figure out how much to share about today's brain glitch. I don't need another ex-boyfriend singling me out as the Woodsdale wacko.

"Fine. Another geocaching run and picnic? You can show me a new park."

"Exactly what I need."

* * *

While we pack our lunch, I describe my non-interview to Geoff. I keep it light.

"I guess I dreamt that call that changed the date." I don't share about my journal and phone calendar—my best means of keeping dreams and reality from meshing. "It's happened before." I shrug. He probably deserves my honesty.

He doesn't comment on my slip up, though. "It'll work out, yeah? You have another opportunity Thursday next."

"I guess so. I hope they don't hold this against me."

"You can't control that. But you're brave to go back and try again."

My throat closes up at his words. They stroke me like gentle fingers.

His smile is sweet, and he seems more relaxed than usual when he puts an arm around me and gives me a squeeze. I lean into the contact. But my nose wrinkles when I smell smoke on his clothes again.

"You'll see. Bakker and her bunch'll be glad to have you," he says. He doesn't mention my dream admission at all, and I flinch since it was the most important detail. And it won't be the last slip he'll see, if he hangs out with me for a while.

* * *

Late in the afternoon, I come home, humming a cheerful tune. Mom confronts me in the kitchen.

"I heard what you told Geoff about missing the interview. You're not having those dreams again, are you?"

I can't believe she would ask that. I put my hands on my hips and scowl at her. "You eavesdropped on me? What's that about? I thought you trusted me to make my own decisions, as an adult.

"And yes, I dream nightly—around five times per night on average. You know this. I remember every dream like it happened while I was wide awake. What makes you think anything has changed? Magic wand syndrome is not attractive to people with disabilities, Mom."

She sighs. "You had no trouble all last quarter. I let myself believe—"Her words trail off and she shakes her head. "Sorry, I was thoughtless. But I didn't mean to overhear your conversation, Tiegen; I just walked past while you were making sandwiches."

"So, it happened again. I got a dream mixed up with real life, okay? But it's no big deal. Dr. Bakker just rescheduled me for later this week."

"Sweetheart, I worry about you. I know the dreams aren't anything you can control. But remember what Dr. Crenshaw told us—about how unique your disorder is. When these mix-ups happen, we need to monitor them and see if your condition worsens. Maybe it's time to check in for an evaluation again."

"Mom, you just pointed out that I've had no trouble in months. That hardly counts as getting worse." I jam the kitchen cabinet open and rustle around in the snack foods, though I'm not hungry.

"Maybe it's time to try a new medication. Or see whether Dr. Crenshaw has new coping ideas. Your dad and I support you in starting your dissertation year a jump ahead of your classmates. Give yourself a good start."

"Okay, stop. One slipup from my dreams and you want to send me back to the loony bin. Or drug me until I drool. Let me remind you, I was my craziest after I took that pre-scription from Dr. Crenshaw. Yuck!"

"Dear, I'm trying to help. I want to make sure you've ex-plored all the routes you can take to keep your disorder un-der control. You might not consider the scarier possibilities on your own. Most of us don't, given a choice."

"Look." I quietly steam, counting out points on my fin-gers. "I do my best, ever, sorting out my dreams from reali-ty; I make a new friend; I look forward to summer for the first time in years; I set up an interview for a job that may be a great fit; and I am already a jump ahead on my disserta-tion. I'm fine, okay?" I hold out my hands and shrug.

"Okay. But keep it in mind. You don't have to deal with this alone."

"That's it. I'm out of here." I stomp to my room, my great afternoon sullied by a flood of anger.

Mom forgets I'm no kid any more. She still sees the past as if it were now. She's clueless about the insights I work in- to my today world. If she's trying to be supportive, I'd much rather have her notice when I excel instead of pointing out my mistakes.

Bleh.

Chapter 7

It's morning. Half-awake, I shift my head and sweep my sleepy eyes over my journal, waiting for my dream dump. Just out of arm's reach. I'm not ready to reach that far. Turning my head is the most I can pull off right now. I close my eyes and glide back toward my sleep haven.

My cellphone rings, but I ignore it. Then the landline rings. Mom peeks in my door and says in a soft voice, "Tiegen?"

It might be Geoff. I quit pretending I'm sleep-deprived, and ease into my day.

"Um-hmm."

"Telephone. An Officer St. Marie?" Her tone rises on the name like it's a question. I look over at eyebrows that arch toward the ceiling.

"Thanks Mom. I'll take it." She hands me the portable landline. I pause, the phone tight against my chest, and display my dismissive smile. She wavers for a moment, then gives in with a grunt and closes the door behind her. Ah, privacy.

"This is Tiegen."

"Hi Tiegen. Jennifer St. Marie here. Did I wake you?"

"No, I'm just not out of bed yet. What's up?"

"Would you give me the phone number of your friend — the one who took the pictures? I'd like to ask him a few questions."

"Um, sure, I guess. Hold on." I grab my cell and pull up Geoff's number. I read it off to the policewoman followed by his name. "He's not in trouble, is he?" My stomach suddenly cramps as I realize I gave out Geoff's phone number without asking him first. This could be bad. Very bad.

"Oh no. I need a better idea of what he saw. That's all. We've heard no news on those men yet — no hate crimes have been reported."

"Good news, I guess." That's the most enthusiasm I can fake as my stomach flip-flops. Oh hell. Why did I give out his number?

"Thanks for the help. I'll tell you if anything comes up. Bye." Jennifer ends the call.

I lie still, encouraging my stomach off of the trampoline, until Geoff calls.

"Hey Tiegen. Did you give Jessica my phone number?"

"Yes. So sorry, I didn't think. She asked, and I just rattled it off like an idiot. Then I realized that you might not want that, but it was too late to take it back." Jabber, jabber, jabber. I press my eyes closed and shut my mouth.

"No worries. Do you know what she wanted?"

My stomach won't unclench. "She said she had questions to ask you. Did she?"

"Yeah, she did. But it was weird. She asked whether I heard those guys say they were going to teach the immigrants a lesson. I told her I was too far away taking pics. Then she asked if I believed what you said you heard."

"Believed me? What did you say?" I'm wide awake now. I even sit up.

"I said of course I did."

Did Geoff sound a bit too forceful? Maybe he doesn't believe me either.

"Why would she ask you that? It sounds like she doubts me."

"I thought the same, though she never said so straight out."

"Well, doesn't that just figure. I wake up deflated. Then a cop manages to treat me like a liar before I even roll out of bed."

"Don't worry. She probably has to double check. Protocol or some such."

"Maybe." My middle is stuck between torture and resolution. I imagine a robed figure inside me with a whip raised to snap the moment I relax.

"But taking that tip to the coppers — Da would say that shows character. You were uncomfortable but chose to do the right thing. I like that."

I sigh softly, so he can't hear. I shake my shoulders and try to flip away my tension. My stomach gurgles.

When we hang up I grab my journal. It seems like I dream about the library men each night now. Most is dreamlike, but bits seem plausible. I worry that dream content could seep into my memories. So I write every detail into my journal. It especially wouldn't do to give the police bogus info.

In addition, I go back and make sure that everything I told Jessica was correct. If dream stuff mixes in, she'll never believe me. Although I flapped my mouth prematurely, everything checks out okay. I got lucky.

* * *

I clean out my daypack. The front pocket holds detritus from the past week, mostly scraps of paper. I scoop it out onto my bed and sort it. Much of the flotsam I toss into the recycle bin—shopping lists, reminders, receipts. Some I set aside to go back into the pack—pens and a notepad, my library card.

Turning it about in my hands, I examine a sheet of folded paper I find tucked between my library card and some notes from earlier in the week. I must have shoved this stuff into my pack in a hurry, because I usually file dissertation info into a special folder before I head home.

I unfold it—it's just a half-sheet—and see scritches in an unfamiliar hand. I look more closely. The page came from a notepad pre-printed with "Woodsdale Athletic Club," its address and a phone number. Beneath that is scrawled a list:

<u>Ibrahim and Mohammad's Lies</u>
Christians are:
>hypocritical
>not devout
>exclusionary
>non-peaceful
>self-centered
>prejudiced

A couple of inches later, there is one more phrase.

Woodsdale Islamic Center!

The exclamation mark blares a klaxon in my brain. I frown and turn the paper over, but it's blank. Abruptly, I recall retrieving papers and my library card after I knocked them onto the floor by Flexman's feet. I must have scooped this up as well. My heart rate increases.

Flexman wrote down the statements made by the guys at his gym — those that he talks about going after. From their names and the place of worship, it sounds like they are Muslims.

I tuck Flexman's note back into the front pocket of my backpack, then add my wallet, library card, and pens. Vindication. I can't wait to show Geoff and Jessica.

I'm flying for the moment, carrying proof that I didn't dream this stuff up. Now Jessica St. Marie has to trust my word. That's important, though I'm still not sure why. And Geoff will see that dreams or not, I can be reliable.

This could be a great day.

* * *

That evening, after I get home from the library, Mom asks what the policewoman called about. I give her the brief version, and don't mention that Jessica may have doubted me. I give Mom my chilly look when she acts concerned. She sighs, but doesn't question me further. I find an excuse to escape to my room before she changes her mind. Where her only child is concerned, her curiosity rarely wanes.

Paranoid that I could have messed up what I remembered, I thumb through my journal again. But I have ordered everything carefully in my neatest handwriting. It's all in the proper columns.

I feel better looking at the ordered columns. I wish that classes would continue through the summer, though. I stay in control of all the details best when I fit them around the framework of a highly structured day.

But that would mean less time with Geoff. And I can barely wait until we are together again. After I journal the details of my day, I get ready for bed. I have Geoff in his Dickensonian cap on my mind.

As I drift to sleep, I replay his delicious kisses. I wouldn't mind dreaming those all night long.

Yum.

* * *

When I see Geoff the next day, I tell him about my find.

"Will you take it to the copper lady then?" He does that thing where he rocks up on his toes.

"What else?"

On the drive over in the car, my senses are inundated with the beauty of Woodsdale. The air comes through the window sweet with lilacs. I glance at Geoff. I easily adopt his high spirits when we're together. And it doesn't hurt that I can prove my statements now, either.

* * *

I look around the interview room Jessica St. Marie has brought us to. Larger than her cubicle, it's still cramped with a desk and the two extra chairs for Geoff and me.

I appreciate being alone with her. Lots of other officers sat at desks in that area where her office was. I had to speak softly out there.

Although the room is stark, the desk holds a photo of Jessica hugging a huge dog, maybe a St. Barnard-Lab mix. She's out of uniform in the picture, dressed in clothes that remind me of Land's End. It's strange to find a personal photo in a room that I suspect multiple officers use. Is she trying to make us comfortable? Bubbles gurgle in my stomach, even though I'm not the suspect here.

At least I don't think I am.

"Why did you question Geoff about my report on the two men?" I take the lead in our meeting.

"I consulted with another officer who wondered whether the reference to hate crimes was real or a prank. With no solid evidence, it was just one person's story. If it were a prank, it could have come from you or from the men you told us about. So I checked with Geoff to see what he knew." Jessica doesn't gloss over her intentions. I respect that.

"I didn't make it up, and I can prove it. I brought a note that I picked up by mistake at the library." I explain how I rediscovered the paper, only then realizing it wasn't one of my own notes.

"Thanks for bringing it in. May I photocopy it for the file?" Jessica asks.

"Of course. It's in my backpack." I unzip the outer pocket of my pack and reach inside. I take out my wallet and set it aside. Then I grab the handful of cards and papers that had mixed themselves together. I tap them on the tabletop to straighten them, and then I flip through the stack. I reach for another handful, but I draw out hard candies, coins, pens, and other small objects. No more paper.

A touch of panic shoots through me. I keep my exterior sedate and fight the urge to wrap my arms around my waist. I am positive that the list was in that pocket. I tell myself not to worry—I must have overlooked it. A caustic burp creeps into the back of my mouth. I swallow it down while I clear my throat.

I stretch wide the exterior pocket and look inside both corners. It's empty. So I return to the first handful of stuff I took out and examine each item for a second time, making certain nothing sticks together.

My breathing speeds up. Sweat seeps out on my face, and I want to wipe it away, but I force myself to open up my wallet instead. There is no paper inside except for a little currency. The list is missing. I repeat my search, rubbing each item between my finger and thumb in case it stuck to something else.

Finally, I can no longer put off the truth by busying my fingers. I have to tell them. "I-I don't know what happened to it. I packed it in this pocket." My voice sounds wheedling. I stop and take a deep breath to still my nausea.

"Maybe it's in the big pocket," Geoff says.

"I'll check." He's trying to help, but I know where I put the paper. Inside the main compartment is my cellphone, a blank tablet, an apple and a few trinkets to leave inside geo-caches. Exactly what I expected and no more.

"Shall I take a look?" he asks.

"Go ahead. But I think it's fallen out, which is weird considering how careful I was with it." I pass him the handful of stuff I took out of the pack and the bag itself. Then I look around on the floor, stand up to shake out my shirt, and check my chair. Nothing. I put my hands into my pockets, then reach down and brush my hand across the seat before sitting again.

"No luck, sorry." Geoff, passes back my daypack and cards.

Jessica hasn't spoken a word while we searched. I fill the silence.

"I guess I didn't bring it after all. Must have left at home. Believe me, it's no prank."

She nods and waits.

I look at Geoff and shrug. He shrugs back. I look back at Jessica.

"Well, at least I told you the details."

"Yes. I've written them down. Is that all for today?"

"Uh, yep. Guess you have other cases to work on." I look at Geoff.

He and I stand up together and turn toward the door. I glance back to see the officer rise as well, but she doesn't show us out.

* * *

"Geoff," I say on the drive back. "Do you think I'm nuts? That I dreamed that piece of paper? What if there never was one? I need to go check my journal and see what I wrote about it."

"Okay." He doesn't respond about whether I'm nuts or not. His face is poker stiff. This isn't good.

I see my hands, white-knuckled on the steering wheel, and come to a decision. "I didn't tell you everything about my dreams. About how hard they make my life. I need to explain. If we spend more time together, you should know in case you don't want to hang around someone with a screwy brain. The missing paper makes me look totally wacko if I don't let you in on my past."

"Go ahead." He doesn't turn his head toward me. "I'm listening."

So I do. I tell him about how I've mixed up real actions and dream actions in the past: neglected homework assignments I dreamed I turned in; friends I accused of saying things that were never spoken; arguments with Mom while I'm fighting-angry and she is clueless; feeling relieved that I made up with my ex-boyfriend only to find him still not speaking to me.

"For most people, dreams are unclear and fade quickly. For me it's like I'm twins—one who fights to live normally—barely holding it together, and the mirror me who has vision, confidence and her sanity intact. Both seem real."

"My dreams have an unreal quality," Geoff says. "So I know they aren't the truth. Even those that seem overpowering when I experience them."

"Right. Mine too. That helps me sort them out." I nod. "But of my four to six nightly dreams, one or two may appear like fragmentary, plausible memories. What really happened is no more real to me than my dreams, so the dreams may cause trouble. I'm liable to see them as real."

I look at him, and he meets my eyes. His tiny smile encourages me.

"When I was a child, before I figured out what was unlikely to be real, anything seemed possible. Monsters, my parents dying, flying, ESP with animals... My folks thought I just exercised a kid's active imagination. But as I grew older, they realized that I had real and fantasy all twisted together."

"That's bloody rotten! You poor kid." Now he's my supporter again. I sit taller.

"I know. When we get home, I'll show you my dream journal and the phone calendar that helps keep me on the right track. They've made a big difference for me over the past few years."

"A clever strategy." His words make me feel even better. I've won him back to my side. For now, at least.

"I don't feel clever right now. And journaling wasn't my idea initially. Mom and Dad took me to dozens of sleep specialists. But a psychiatrist suggested the journal and calendar."

"It's still brilliant that you use it."

"When it works, I guess. But did I dream that piece of paper? Or some of the things the men said? Maybe everything I told the officer was dream imagery. I don't know what to believe. It doesn't take much to jar my confidence. Once, I even dreamed that I had checked my journal and that everything was right when it wasn't. At times like that, I'm sure that I'm crazy."

"No wonder you disliked having Jessica question your statement."

"Yeah. Not one of my best moments. And dreaming the interview had been rescheduled, that really stank. In my journal, nothing suggested I'd learned that from a dream. It was a routine detail that I never questioned—just changed it on my calendar." I shake my head.

We arrive home then, and Geoff draws me into a close hug. Then he brushes the hair out of my face and looks deep into my eyes. Our lips press together, and I lean against him.

"You're fine as you are. I don't kiss daft women, I promise."

"I could be dreaming this too, for all I know."

"Then I'll kiss you every day until you believe it's real."

* * *

I let Geoff read my latest journal and compare it to my calendar. All my recent blunders are outlined there—more than I admit to anyone. I usually swing with little ones in the moment. Thank goodness for an awesome imagination.

I recognize the confused looks when I cast misinformation into a conversation. At times I can pretend I misspoke and restate thoughts immediately—my successful episodes.

While he peruses the pen and paper part of my brain, I can't help thinking about the things I've written there about him. If it weren't for the dream issue, I wouldn't be letting him see that stuff. But I have to hide things every day in life. I'd rather not do it with a guy I care about.

Still, I watch him through the corner of my eye to see if his face changes at those parts. Once he chuckles, and despite my great ideals about transparency, I blurt, "What's that?" As usual, my stomach starts to ache.

"I wasn't aware of my 'quaint word usage.' Comes from not being on this side of the pond long enough to pick up the local idiom, I suppose." I can tell he's hoping for reassurance.

"Don't feel awkward," I say, describing my own state as much as his. I force myself to meet his eyes. "I appreciate our differences. Listening to people from the UK is a pleasure for most of us in the States. Like the people at the brewery."

"I'll take it as a compliment then. Especially if you take me to a party or two and prove it to me." He smiles.

"That would be difficult." I don't want him to know how my disability prevents me from invites out with my peers. I change what I'm about to say.

"Everyone would try to steal you away from me!" That makes him laugh. Then he reads on. I know he'll find more descriptions of himself, and my stomach kicks me with a steel-toed boot. Silently, I tell my stomach to shove it.

To distract myself, I search again for the slip of paper that I so carefully slipped into my backpack. At first, I keep half my attention on Geoff, but then I get a little wild. I tear through everything on my desk, shake out my duvet and put it back on the bed, peer under the furniture, pick through my dirty laundry for pocket contents, and empty my waste basket on the floor before sorting everything back inside, including lumps of already-been-chewed gum. Just my luck—if the paper is real, it is truly lost.

Frustrated, I sit hard onto my mattress and it bounces. I glance up and see Geoff's stricken expression. He closes my journal and moves over to sit beside me. At first I think he saw a comment that he disliked, and my gut protests again.

"I hate seeing you go through this," he says. "It's really horrid, isn't it?"

I gulp and nod and try to hold back tears that leap to my eyes. "I'm constantly on the alert for escaped dream bits. It takes a lot of self-control and a fair amount of time. I'm always scared I'll slip up."

He puts an arm around me and kisses my eyes. When he moves down to my mouth, we both lay back on the bed. His body against mine makes me feel sane. It's real. Completely real.

"Will you write about this kiss?" he asks.

I smile again. I want to stay here in my room where nothing can go awry.

Well, that and feel Geoff's body against mine.

* * *

After Geoff leaves, I search again for the slip of paper. I throw off the bedding, move all the furniture, pull the mattress onto the floor, take out and put back everything on the floor of my closet even though I'm certain I didn't open it after finding Flexman's notepad page. No luck.

Now what? I could tell Jessica St. Marie that I may have dreamed it, or say I made it up, or just continue as if I'm certain about its existence. Doing nothing seems easiest, but that's a rare freedom—it too often backfires. I don't want another dream mire if I can avoid it.

Here I thought that I had my disability in hand, only to have two major mishaps within a week. My loss of control stabs my gut. More than one of my specialists told me that I am as limited by this feeling, and the poor self-image that accompanies it, as I am by my dreams. I have trouble believing it. They don't have to live in my world, where friends are few and lonely days contain too much time to second guess myself. How can they know?

I sit up straight, take deep breaths, look at the mirror me, and repeat affirmations like Dr. Crenshaw taught me. *I suc-*

ceed at the challenges that come my way. School is easy for me. I will earn my Ph.D. by the end of next year. Geoff likes me.

The drill sergeant still stands in the pit of my stomach, but he's less active. Maybe I should let Jennifer know about the dreams. Or maybe I can double check whether my information is correct or not.

I pick up my cell and call Geoff.

"Hey. I need to make sure the piece of paper from Flexman was real. I want to check whether the gym on the stationary exists. Maybe we can visit there—pick up a clue."

"I'm up for anything. When?"

* * *

It's Wednesday morning, and Geoff and I head to the fitness center at the address on the now missing piece of paper. Attempting to form a clear picture of the paper in my mind didn't yield the address, but at least a place with the name I remembered came up on the Internet with all the info I needed.

We park at the gym and study the outside first. Nothing special here. Geoff elbows me in the side, and when I look over, he gives me an "after you" gesture.

Inside, a woman in professional attire at the main desk beams at us. "Good morning," she says. As expected, we can't pass her surreptitiously, so we approach the counter.

"We want to check out your facility." I encouraged Geoff to speak because of his lovely accent. Might as well charm the heck out of them. "We're looking for a place to work out over the summer until college starts."

Her smiling mouth grows even wider. It looks unreal. "Wait just a moment, and I'll find you a guide for the grand tour."

She talks briefly on the phone, and soon a ripped blond dude arrives to shake our hands. His six-pack abs show through his thin t-shirt, and he stands in an unnatural way that shows off his muscles. I wonder if he points like that guy on TV who shows off his biceps, and I force down a snicker.

He asks about our interests, and identifies himself, with some pride, as a personal trainer. Every few minutes, he tosses back his head to get his too-long bleached bangs out of his face.

We trail him down the corridor.

"That chap is certainly full of himself," Geoff whispers, and winks.

"His name should be Schwarzenegger," I whisper back. "He thinks he's a hunk."

"I wouldn't mind looking that solid, though."

"Nah. You're fine the way you are." It seems like Geoff stands a little taller after that.

Throughout the tour, I search for Flexman. No go. He's not here. What are the chances that we'd pick the same time to come as he does? Still, we smile and nod at Schwarzenegger and encourage him onward.

"May we see the locker rooms?" Geoff asks, and Schwarzenegger recites the appropriate advertising as he leads us to them. I'm glad that he can't follow me into the women's. I look around inside mainly so I can escape for a few. The drinking fountain is a nice way to waste one more minute. I giggle and reset my face before I step back out.

Afterwards, in a featureless office, Schwarzenegger gives the sales pitch of the month with the yearly fee and how it transfers to another facility when we move. I swear I see dollar signs in his azure eyes.

"Sorry we took up your time, then. As we told you earlier, the next three months is all we want," says Geoff. "A year-long membership would be a waste." He stands and I do the same.

"I can arrange for a three-month membership," the hunk replies quickly.

"If you cared about us as potential clients, you wouldn't have given us a one-year spiel before offering us the three months we asked for." I throw that over my shoulder as we walk to the exit. Just before we step outside, I stop and look back.

Schwarzenegger blinks a couple of times, probably dislodging his money-colored lenses now that his oh-so-certain sale is walking out. Then he slides open a drawer. "To show you that we care, I have free one-week guest passes for you both. Come work out and I guarantee that you'll return." He extends the cards with a sweep of his hand. "Get these punched at the counter when you enter."

"Thanks. We'll try it." I snatch the passes. "By the way, what are your busiest times of day?" I rejoin Geoff at the exit, where he holds the door open. We exit, and Schwarzenegger parks himself in the doorway. He watches me unlock the car.

"Early morning and evening. Afternoon is a great if you like fewer customers. See you both tomorrow?"

* * *

In the afternoon, I do my studying so I can pay attention again tonight at the library. On Monday and Tuesday, I repeated my charade with the earbuds but no music. Although the two men griped to each other, they didn't mention actions they planned to take or identify people they wanted to hurt. I'm beginning to think I'm wasting my time here. It was just talk.

So when I'm seated at the always-empty table by the guys, I really don't expect to hear much. I expect I might even get some more reading in.

But tonight, I'm wrong.

Chapter 8

In the midst of their conversation, Flexman leans toward Baldy and speaks more softly than usual.

"I've been collecting a little data. I followed one of those leeches today. I found out where he lives. Tomorrow I'll track the other one."

"You really did? Man, you've got balls."

Then the conversation becomes so soft for a few minutes that I can't make out their words. Finally, they go back to their usual routine and say no more about the men from the gym.

I leave before Flex and Baldy do, and wait in my car for them to come out when the library closes. I'm going to follow Flexman to his house. I've got to tell Jessica that these guys might try something violent this weekend. At least if I know where Flex lives, the cops may be more likely to follow through this time.

When Flex and Baldy walk out of the library, I slip down in the seat until my head is below the dash board. Although my stomach immediately gets achy, I count to ten before I peek again. I don't want them to recognize me, or know this is my car.

When I chance a look around the parking lot, I see Flex slide into a van and pull it out onto the street. I let one car pass, then pull out behind it, and follow the cars to the light on the corner. I think I'm doing a great job until the light turns just as Flexman crosses the intersection. The car before me stops for the red, and I watch Flex's car drive down the street and turn a corner.

"Crap. I lost him." I slap the steering wheel.

When the light changes, I take the same route, but as I turn the corner, I can see that Flex has vanished. Part of me is angry that I didn't plan better. Part of me is glad I lost him. Tailing someone's car is harder than it looks on TV.

Maybe that's a good thing.

* * *

The next morning, at the gym, I put on a tight workout tee hoping Geoff will like it on me. He doesn't look half bad in his workout clothes. He has left his cap at home.

"Shall we give the weight machines a go?" he asks.

"Sure."

While we take turns on the machines, we are mostly alone. That gives us a chance to talk.

"Later this morning I have my job interview redux."

"You'll do great."

"It seems that I already have, just from my resume and application. My new confirmation letter came yesterday, and it contained a P.S." I strike a pose and recite for him. "'Although all applicants must attend an interview, we are impressed by your application. The interview is mostly a formality. We hope you will make a great addition to our team.'"

"Terrific news!" Geoff raises a hand and we high-five.

A warm shiver runs through me.

* * *

Again, I give myself plenty of time. I arrive a little early, well-dressed for my interview. Four other applicants sit in the room with me while Dr. Bakker, whom I spoke with last week, presents an overview of the position, the ongoing re-search, and the possible duties of the successful candidate. Turns out she's the director.

Figures.

I absorb every word, attracted by the position. The first step, using a set screening interview on potential research subjects over the phone, seems like something I couldn't mess up. And I like independent work, because I'm less like-ly to make a dream content error in conversation.

This is a perfect job for me. I know it.

After the presentation, they call us, one at a time, into a room with three people inside, one of whom is Dr. Bakker. They introduce themselves, and I give my special apprecia-tive smile to the woman whose signature is on my letter. They ask a few questions, and I do my best to give thorough, thoughtful replies. Then they ask what I'd like to know. I talk about some of the things that excite me about the job us-ing words I practiced in my mind while I awaited my turn. I can tell they are impressed. To cinch it, I turn to Dr. Bakker.

"I was excited when I read your letter. Especially the P.S. I feel less nervous today, knowing that I am a top candidate for the job. I promise—you will be glad you selected me."

Suddenly, reality shifts. If I were standing, I believe the floor would have bucked me off of my feet like something from an Indiana Jones movie. Could this be a dream?

The managers suddenly freeze, their expressions melting into scapes of confusion, irritation and anger. What happened? I glance at my chest in case I had a wardrobe mal-function, but my clothes are all in place. I look up again, while a large rodent nibbles my stomach lining.

Dr. Bakker looks most angry. In fact, seeing her red face and bulging eyes, I fear she might take out a scimitar and whop my head off. I suddenly see the scene where Jones is given monkey brains served in the skull. I gulp.

"I wrote no such thing," Dr. Bakker says. "No letters included a P.S. They were identical except for the applicant's name and the meeting dates. Nor have we pre-determined who is likely to be hired." I hear her continue in my imagination, "but it certainly won't be you!" I shut down that part of my brain and go into rescue mode.

"You know, I looked forward to this day so much, I bet I dreamed that P.S. Please excuse me. It must have been wishful thinking. Truly, I'd be inspired to contribute to your research."

"Like you dreamt coming on the wrong day last week?" Dr. Bakker says.

Uh oh. I forgot I already told the truth once. Second time around, I always need to lie. There's no third strike with my dream disability.

"Yes. Like that. I've thought of little else," I conclude like an idiot. The look on the third woman's face has changed to what? Pity? It doesn't get much worse than that. "May I answer any other questions for you? I'd be glad to share some of the ideas I..."

"That's all." The director's tone is brusque and she doesn't even look my way. "Find your own way out?"

My throat closes up, so I can only nod and bolt. I barely reach the car before I explode into acid tears of defeat.

* * *

I call Officer Jessica when I get home.

"You know that paper with info on it about the hate crime the library guy was planning? I couldn't find it. I wonder if maybe I dreamed it." I give a little laugh to make this seem less of a big deal, but it sounds fake.

"Does that mean that the information was inaccurate?"

"I still believe it's real, but I can't help but doubt myself since I can't find the stupid thing." Frustration leaks into my words.

"And the two men in the photograph—they said the things you told me earlier?"

"Yes. I'm quite certain about that. I checked my journal where I'd written it all down the night it happened."

"What does that mean—that you wrote it in your journal?"

"I write down important stuff there. For reference." I choose my words carefully. I'm certain I don't want to let her know about how I mix dream content into reality. It would make me seem flakey—a totally unreliable witness. Of course, at times, that's correct.

"But you didn't copy from the missing slip of paper into your journal?"

"That's in there, too, paraphrased. It's just--"

"Yes?"

"I'm unsure because I can't find the paper." I'm toying with a trap that may snap closed on me at any instant.

Jessica just waits, quiet on the other end of the phone.

My abdomen cramps and I wince. "You don't believe me, do you?" I wonder why I made this call.

"It's hard to know what to believe. You and Geoff saw the men at the library, so I assume they exist. And on your first trip to the station, you seemed clear about what you heard. You sounded frightened."

"I was scared. You're right."

"But beyond that, I keep an open mind. Something is going on, and I doubt you've given me the whole story. As an officer, I distrust that."

"There is something I can't tell you, true. But it regards my own issues, not the guys at the library, I promise." As soon as the words jump out of my mouth, I realize I haven't told her about trying to shadow Flexman. This would not be a good time, so I hold that knowledge in reserve since I never got close to finding out where he lives.

"But last night, Flexman bragged that he'd followed one guy home, and he planned to follow the other one home, today."

"Did he say what else he planned to do?"

"No, that was it."

"Okay then. Keep in touch. Tell me as much as you can. Right now, I can't take any action except to see if other information turns up." She doesn't say this in a hurtful way. I believe she will help if she can. But I sure wish I had Flexman's address for her.

"I will tell you almost everything," I say. It's the only promise I can honestly give her. But I mean it.

Even if it means following Flex home.

Chapter 9

"How did your job interview go?" It's the first thing Mom asks when she sees me.

"Not great. I didn't get the job." My voice sounds like fatigue with the flu.

"Oh sweetie, that's a shame. I know how much you wanted it."

Mom puts an arm around me. I had planned to pass it off as something everybody has to put up with. But suddenly, fifteen years drop off my age, and I just want to be held like a child with a scraped knee. I turn to hug her and her arms are strong and secure. Immediately my tears erupt again.

"What happened sweetheart? Tell me about it," Mom says as she reaches up to massage my back like she did when I was a kid.

And I don't even try to protect myself. I tell her about the letter and the P.S. that didn't exist. How all the expressions of support and friendliness morphed into ugliness, and how tersely Dr. Baker dismissed me.

Mom holds me for a long time. She strokes my hair and mutters motherish words that gradually soothe.

"I can't believe I was so stupid." I heave a final sob.

"Look, sweetheart, you were right about how well you did last quarter. I let my fears for you interfere with telling you how proud I am. You handled your disability like the adult you are. Maybe having dream incursions twice around this job means that somehow the job wasn't right for you."

I ponder this. We drift into the living room, my hand in hers, and sit together on the couch.

"No, it was perfect for me. I would have learned so much. If anything, that may have kept it in my dreams—hoping too hard."

"Yet your dreams sabotaged your chances of getting the job," Mom says.

Sabotage. I hate that word.

"I haven't thought about it that way, but all that dream content comes out of my own brain. It's more like I'm two people—me, and the dream me that I see in the mirror. She seems clearer than me, more brightly colored, and so sure of herself, while my life is a fog of insecurity. There have been times I thought my dream self was evil, but I don't think so anymore. I envy her, having it all together. When I'm busy doing things outside of my norm, that's when her reality mixes into mine."

"Well, with graduation, the job interview, your new boy-friend..."

"Mom!"

"Good things can still be stressors, sweetie."

"I know. But Geoff's more than just a good thing. He makes me truly happy. Happier than I was last year."

"I'm glad. Hopefully, more time with him will make up a little for missing out on the research internship. Have you told him about your dreams?"

"Yes. He believes in me, despite them. He acts no different than if I wore a hearing aid. He looks right past it to where I am. The real me, you know?"

"That's wonderful. I hope it works out well for you both." Mom means it—I can tell.

"I've been thinking about what you said, about how I should get another psych work-up done. Maybe you're right. I might get new ideas on how to handle the dreams so stuff like this doesn't happen again."

"You think about it, dear. We can set it up whenever you want. Don't do it just because I pushed so hard the other day. I didn't think clearly. Even when you've been an adult for years, you can say things you regret. I love you so much."

"Thanks Mom." I give her another hug before I go to my room to consider my disordered life. The me in the mirror looks worried too.

* * *

"How was the interview?" Geoff's question is déjà vu. So I tell the story again.

He whistles. "What rot! It's like you set yourself up to fail on it. Yet I know you wanted that job."

I sigh. "That's what Mom said, too. I don't like thinking that way. It means I could sabotage any part of my life through my dreams. What if I blew my dissertation defense? Or chased you away?"

"You won't." He said it like a fact. And although he couldn't know for sure, I felt better.

"I'll have to work on that piece. Maybe see what my psychiatrist says."

"Do it. The journaling works, right? She might have other good ideas."

"Yeah. You're right." I decide to change the subject.

"If Flexman works regular hours, he has to work out in the morning or between work and the library. What if we try for a really early start at the gym tomorrow?"

"Let's go at 7:00 in the a.m. He shouldn't have come and gone that early."

"I feel tired just planning it, but you're right. I have a hard time believing I was getting up that early for classes just a week ago."

He gazes at me with — is that affection?

"Why don't you skip the library tonight. Take a break with me. We can kick back and watch TV together," Geoff says.

"Great idea. Relieve some stress."

"Righto. I never planned to play detective — wrings me out." He leads me into the living room. We cuddle close together on the couch.

"Last night, Flex said he'd followed home one of the men from the gym. So I tried to follow him home, but I lost him at the first stoplight."

"Next time, let me drive. Learning from your experience, I bet I could pull it off."

"You have a license?"

"A UK one."

"If you want to follow someone while driving an unfamiliar car on the wrong side of the street, go ahead. Sounds like an exciting ride."

"I like a challenge."

"Usually, I do too. Like getting my Ph.D."

"That's good, since life throws one a lot of challenges."

"You see how my dreams trip me up. That's what I'm terrified of. I'm more relaxed when I'm not around people much. I liked that research opportunity, where I'd mainly work alone on the phone. It's hard to get in trouble when I read from a script and otherwise keep my mouth closed."

"I rather like your mouth." He draws me into a kiss.

I push away abruptly. "Yuck!"

"What?" He grabs my hands and looks into my eyes. "Are you okay?"

"You taste like ashes." I look around for a place to spit, but it appears I've neglected to outfit the room with a cuspidor.

For the first time since I've known him, Geoff looks irritated.

"That's all? You acted cool with my using green."

"I'm not, really." That's hard to admit. I realize I just made it worse by not telling him sooner. "But I figured it wasn't my business. I thought I'd adjust to the smell on your clothes. I was working on that. But I never kissed a smoker before. I'm sorry, but it was gross."

"But I gave up the cigs. It's just..."

"A little green. I know." I let my tone tell him it was not little to me.

"Don't get sarcastic with me!"

We stare at each other in shock, each broadcasting irritation, neither saying anything for a minute or so. I am flustered, not wanting to fight, but knowing I won't adjust to smoke-bitter kisses either.

Finally, I take a deep breath and ask, "Is this our first fight?"

He sighs. "It doesn't have to be. Can we take a pause until tomorrow? We can go to the gym like we planned. If you still want to."

"Yes."

"Okay. See you then."

Not glancing back, he walks out. The latch of the door sounds accusing.

Chapter 10

The next morning, our contentiousness seems past. I am overly careful not to make Geoff out to be the bad guy, and I don't mention his cannabis use. He doesn't smell of pot, and I'm sure he won't taste of it either. Even his pupils look normal. I appreciate the gesture. It means peace for the moment, though I know the issue isn't settled.

When we reach the athletic club the place looks like we've slipped through a black hole into another dimension. It's packed with people showing off their muscles in expensive workout clothes — a holding tank for narcissists. Instead of concentrating on fitness, a group of people cycle through the rooms about every fifteen minutes, their eyes checking out each profile.

I have on a solid blue tee and new, though practical, shorts. I want to pass under the radar. After surveying the wolf pack, I fear I'm an eyesore no one could ignore. I should have dressed up more.

In the corner, I find an older model treadmill with basic settings that nobody else is likely to want, and hide there, exercising while I wait. I shudder when the looky-loos file through, and I try to do invisible.

"I'm going to try the weight machines again." Geoff leaves. The machines are in the other room, but I'm fine with that. We'll take in more of what's happening if we hang in different places.

Then I see Flexman. He saunters into the room and glances around, checking out the people along with his reflection in the mirrors. I hadn't imagined him as part of the meat market culture – he's not much of a looker, though he has the duds.

I jerk the tie out of my hair so it falls over my face, and I duck my head so he can't see who I am. Hopefully my outfit will be enough of a turnoff to make me forgettable.

In my mind, I hear Flexman's inflammatory tenor from the library again: "First I follow each one home. Then bam!" I sure don't want to get on his hate list. I bite my lip and duck. It's a long moment before I glance up.

Flex is aboard an elliptical, two rows in front of mine, on the other side of the room. He pushes a few buttons and the machine moves. Once he's situated, I step off my treadmill, pick up my towel, and escape, keeping my head down. I move with quick, furtive steps.

I find Geoff chinning himself on a cross bar.

"Geoff?"

With a little kick, he swings away from the bar and lands on the floor.

"What's up? You're shaking!"

"Flexman is in the next room, where I just was." I speak softly and hope only Geoff hears me.

"You'd best stay away from there—he'll recognize you." Geoff's voice is quick—choppy. "Take my place here, and I'll take a station within earshot of him. I doubt he noticed me at the library. I'll be just another stranger."

"Okay." My shoulders release once I know I will be out of Flexman's sight. I shake off the shivers and stand taller.

But now that he will be in Flex's view, I worry about Geoff. Again I hear Flexman's words in my memory: "Somebody should hand them a teaching."

"Don't do anything risky." But Geoff doesn't seem to hear me. He talks in a pressured voice.

"I want to follow him into the locker room when he's finished. I bet that's where the conversations took place that you heard him mention. So we may be here awhile. Do you mind?"

"That's fine. Grab me when the coast is clear, okay? I'll find a seat in the lobby by the juice bar when I've showered. Hey, do you think we could follow him home?"

"Will do." Geoff heads for the cardio machines.

I work the weight circuit, letting the exercise stretch the tension out of my shoulders, but my mind seems immune. I can't stand not knowing what's happening. I look up at the clock and wonder if it is faulty. Surely it is creeping along in slow motion. I move on to the next challenge. After fifteen minutes, I give myself permission to walk past the windows to the cardio room, which is full of people. I see Geoff's back in the row behind Flexman's. I doubt he'll hear anything worthwhile since nobody's talking. Most eyes tune to individual TV screens.

I return to my circuit, having to wait my turn to get back in the equipment loop. I really dislike being so visible, but I focus on my repetitions, and try to keep from looking at the clock every minute. Or in the mirror.

At three more quarter-hour intervals, I check the cardio room again. On the last pass through, both Geoff and

Flexman are missing. My curiosity balloons, and I hear my midsection gurgle.

Time to clean up and move to my next position. Do real spies have sour stomachs, too? I hurry through my shower and dress so I'll be done before the guys. Then I go out to the juice bar, where people sit, drinking hideous green smoothies as they flirt together.

I make a face, and then find a health magazine to hide behind. I plant myself in a chair where I can see everyone as they come and go. Behind the magazine I wait, turning random pages. The sculpted people in the magazine dress suspiciously like the crowd here. Where do ordinary humans go to exercise? I shake my head, feeling more out of place than ever.

Figure after figure pass in and out of the gym. I turn page after page in the magazine.

But I jump, stifling a gasp, when Flexman finally appears. I move the magazine closer to my face, and freeze behind it like a startled rabbit.

If he recognizes me, I'm in major trouble.

Chapter 11

After a moment, I peek out from the side of the magazine with one eye. I hold my breath. Flexman's on autopilot, though, unaware of me. He moves quickly forward into the rest of his day. Once the door closes behind him, I put down the magazine, and meander toward the door. I glance out, looking for his aging white van.

Almost immediately, Geoff joins me, and we head for my car, keeping out of sight. Before we reach the car, I see the van with exhaust blowing from the back pipe. Flex's about to back out.

"What happened inside?" I shoot my thumb back at the gym

"I saw him, but I couldn't identify the men he disliked. Nor did his friend from the library show up. The locker room was crowded, and he didn't speak to anyone that I noticed."

Geoff pulls the car out of the parking lot, following Flex's van.

I gesture with my chin at a dark-haired man leaving the facility as we drive past it. "I wonder if he could be one of the potential victims."

"Who knows? He looks the part."

"Did Flex see you?"

"Yes, but I saw no sign he recognized me. I'm just part of the background here. But I worry about him seeing you. If he thinks about it, he'll recognize you from the library, and wonder how you suddenly turned up elsewhere in his life."

"Now that he's seen you, you better make sure that he doesn't notice you following him." I look at Geoff, and he nods.

"Don't worry. I'll lose him before I'll let him see me." Geoff let a couple of cars pull out between our two vehicles.

As we near the stop light, it turns yellow. I grip my purse. Geoff veers into the far lane, and speeds up to pass through the same light as Flexman. We zip through just before the light turns red, though my foot stomps on a non-existent brake pedal, twice.

Geoff drops back again, on alert for the next stop light. Soon afterward, the van turns onto a residential street. Geoff breaks farther back, while I stare out the window. If I can keep my eyes on the van, maybe it won't vanish. I wish I had a gas pedal now. I'd get closer. My heart sprints, and in my peripheral vision I see my hand, on the dash board, knuckles white.

The van turns into a driveway about a block ahead of us. As we come close, it pulls into a garage and the garage door auto-closes. I jot down the house number and laugh. "You did it!" My voice is too loud for the inside of a car.

Geoff slaps the steering wheel in glee. He's more amped than I am, I think, but we're both celebratory — talking fast.

He continues past the house.

"I don't think he saw us, do you?" I have to make sure.

"No worries. We're good." His face is full of sunshine.

"Cool. I guess I finally have some information for Officer Jessica — his address. I'll give her a call before she leaves tonight. That should make it easier for the police to keep an eye on him this weekend."

"That it should. And while the police take over, we can forget about Flex and have a great weekend together, if you want."

"More geocaches, parks, and breweries?"

"Sure. Or TV and cuddles. We can see how we feel."

He drives to my place, and stops the car in the driveway.

"I'm sorry I wasn't nicer yesterday about the pot. I never meant to fight with you."

"I don't want to fight either."

"Do you mind telling me what you get from smoking it? I want to understand."

"I don't mind. Cannabis relaxes me. You've probably noticed that I'm nervy at times. I don't want that to get out of hand. Grass really helps. When I'm mellow I take more time to think problems through. And it makes me more comfortable around people. Like with you, it would have been really hard for me to ask you out without a few puffs. I mean, it's not my country, and I don't know how things work here. Even at home, I'm no natural with the women. I don't want to make an idiot of myself."

"Okay, I can see that." I nod, surprised that he's more like me that I realized.

"Also, it keeps me from wanting cigs. Bad habit, that. Plus, I like the creativity I feel when I'm high. And how delectable everything looks — and tastes." His words take on more color. "I notice so much more with all my senses! You should see the light on the leaves — it's indescribable."

"Oh." That's way too much to ask him to give up. "I-I don't know what to say. But I have to tell you, it tasted vile. For me, it ruined our kiss."

"Yeah, well—I'll figure out something—carry a tooth-brush or some mints."

"That would be excellent." I tell myself to work harder at getting used to the scent on his clothing.

"But I'm surprised you never tried it. You drink beer. Did you ever try cigs?"

"Once, when I was a kid. They made me sick. I coughed until I puked. Never again!" I laugh. "That was a quick les-son. I can't imagine pot would be any easier."

"It can be harsh to inhale until you get used to it. But you know you don't have to smoke the stuff, right? They have it available in edibles. You can't know you'd dislike something you've never sampled."

"It's not just smoking that's an issue. My brain is screwed up already. Over the years, doctors have tried all kinds of meds on me. None helped dampen down the dreams. Most had awful side effects. Some made me feel distant, like I wasn't really here. Others made the dreams worse. One gave me hallucinations. And those were FDA regulated medica-tions at researched dosages. Cannabis isn't dose controlled. I've gotten to hate all drugs."

"I didn't realize."

"My psychiatrist told me that there appears to be a corre-lation between people who use cannabis and those who have psychotic episodes, too. It's not a great idea for anyone with a disability like mine."

"Yeah. I get that."

"But I sure don't want to miss out on kissing you."

At that, he leans over in the seat and kisses me thorough-ly, right there in front of the house.

I don't even care if the neighbors see.

Chapter 12

In Saturday's mail, I get an impersonal postcard stating that I was not chosen for the research position. Though I knew I'd been dropped, the card brings back, with enhanced visual effects, my humiliating interview. My mood drops into the gutter. I consider the possible benefit of checking in for a mental exam again, but I'm just not ready. Surely, I'm not that bad off. Or am I?

Wetas gnaw my stomach lining. What might I learn if I went? Maybe I'm certifiable already and only appear to hold it together well enough to pass as normal. I don't want to get labeled. But I don't want to lose control in public, either. Could that happen? Would marijuana make it worse?

I look up schizophrenia in the **Diagnostic and Statistical Manual V** online and count my symptoms. The results neither reassure me nor convince me of my insanity. As usual, answers about my mental health are indecisive. My case doesn't fit any diagnosis. I balance on the edge of mental illness where the footing is crumbly, moss-covered shale. I blank my mind to the possibilities, all of which seem ominous.

To distract myself, I pick up a stack of paper on my desk and take it to my bed: mail, notes to myself, papers I need to file. I get out three folders and label them "To File," "Deal with ASAP," and "Other." I sort stuff into the files. When I come to something I no longer need, I crumple it into a tight wad and toss it toward my wastebasket across the room. A few end up inside, but the throwing itself is therapeutic. I throw harder and harder until I bounce the trash off the wall, my desk, the wastebasket, the floor and even the window. I gather up the misses and throw them again and again until the tension in my body releases.

Then I put the folders back on my desk, and round up the remaining paper lumps from off of the floor before dropping back on my bed with a sigh, my surge of emotion passing.

I can't help thinking how much better life would be as the woman in my mirror. I envy her clarity, her sureness, her stability. She'd never need a psych eval. I groan. Helpless.

It's good that I'm going to spend the rest of the weekend with Geoff. Maybe I can get past my double interview screw up. Cast it out of my brain.

I'm really tired of thinking about it.

* * *

Tuesday morning, I have a dental check-up, something I put off during finals. By going to the earliest appointment in the morning, I climb out of bed a little early, feeling like I've captured an extra few hours for my day.

The appointment goes well. I am consistent about my oral health. The dentist compliments me on my daily dental routine, which feels great.

Driving home, I realize I'm near the gym, and that it's nearly the time when Geoff should be leaving. I see his bike out front when I drive up, so I park in the shopping center lot across the way where I can watch from concealment, just in case Flexman comes out while I wait.

I pop in my earbuds, and settle back.

Geoff is probably right about our mystery. I mean, Flexman probably just has a diarrhea mouth, with no follow-through. Our investigation sure hasn't turned up much. I doubt the gym will yield more than the library has.

At that moment, Geoff walks through the gym doors with a spectacular redhead in a black body wrap t-shirt with holes carefully torn to peek-a-boo her skin. I snort at the obviousness of the style. Fake, but I have to admit, sexy. Fits with all the pheromones that fly around in that building.

Geoff bends down towards the woman, who looks up at him through enough eye make-up to take the place of a Mardi Gras mask. *Is he? No. It can't be!* He kisses her once, twice, and again. Then one of his arms pulls her closer, and he fingers flesh through one of the tears.

Her arms encircle him, too, and for several minutes, they appear to have no consciousness of anything but one another. She rubs up against him in an erotic way.

I can't watch anymore. The poison darts that missed my heart tear open my stomach, spilling acid throughout my body. I think even my legs are going to throw up.

I take a deep breath and hold it while I start the car and drive out toward home. I study only the road. I don't care if Geoff sees the car — in fact, I hope he will. Serve him right.

I get all the way around the corner before I have to pull over and puke in someone's rock-garden parking strip.

* * *

At home, I close myself into my room and cry into my pillow. Eventually, I guess I fall asleep, because the doorbell wakens me. I know it has to be Geoff. It's the time we had arranged to meet here.

Suddenly, I'm so angry with him I think I may rip him to pieces with my claws and teeth like a panther. I bound to the door and fling it wide.

There he stands, looking just the same as always, cute little cap, open face—no sign that he's seeing someone else, or that he noticed my car near the gym. I watch as a quizzical look forms on his familiar features. Then he appears concerned for me. Before, I loved that look on his face. Now it makes me want to shriek.

"What's up, Tiegen?" He tries to step inside.

I block him.

"Don't you dare come into my house! How can you pretend that everything is fine?"

"What—what are you talking about? I just got here. Is this about the green again? I took clean clothes to the gym and showered before coming over."

"I saw you, out in front of the gym this morning. You and that sex-pot in rags."

"Who? What?" He shakes his head slowly. His eyebrows knit tight above his eyes.

"I was driving home from the dentist's, saw it was about time for you to leave the gym, and stopped by to see if you'd gotten new information. But you weren't even looking for Flexman. You only had eyes for that girl. And hands, and lips..."

My mouth trembles and my gut twists painfully. I don't want to cry. I try to surf the wave of my anger.

"I don't know who kissed whom, but I wasn't involved. I assure you, I'm not that man!"

"Don't lie. I saw you two in the sunlight. Just this morning. Did you meet her there? I suppose she doesn't mind if you've been smoking grass? Is she why you want me to stay away from the gym?"

"Now wait a minute. That's not fair. I'm going to the gym to protect you from being seen. So why were you were spying on me? What kind of paranoid behavior is that? First you think there are terrorists in the library. Next you think I am kissing some girl at the gym? "

"No fair turning my fears against me. I am not crazy. I'm pissed!"

"You think I didn't notice?"

"So you act however you want and then pretend innocence when I catch you. Yes, I took a chance at honesty and shared what's going on with me, even though I know it isn't flattering. But I wouldn't have said a word if I'd known it would come back as ammunition against me."

"Okay, maybe I overstepped the bounds a little. But it was self-protective. Because I'm the one being attacked unfairly here."

"I know what I saw."

"Did you dream all this? Because I swear, it never happened."

Through my anger, a little mouse of doubt creeps in. Did I dream this? My feeling of betrayal is linked to my expectation that Geoff wouldn't act in this way. Was I right about that? My brain scrambles for reality markers I can tie it to.

"D-dreamed it?" I try for haughty indignation, but my words betray me. The more I think about it, the more likely a dream seems. Crap. Am I the one who is acting irresponsibly?

"M-maybe so. I didn't stop to think it through."

"That's the first decent thing you've said. Maybe you should've considered it before assuming I was cheating on you. You think?" He glares at me.

Just as I'm about to tell him I'm sorry, that touch of sarcasm feeds my anger once again.

"How can I be sure you're not just using my dreams as an excuse to sneak around?"

"Bollocks!" Geoff casts his fists toward the ground as his chin comes up. Then he takes a breath and squints at me for a moment. After a pause, he speaks through his locked front teeth.

"Look. I've done my best to be understanding, but I'm not going to take this shite from you. Let's leave it go. I don't need abuse from you or anyone else!"

Before I can apologize, he is gone. The sound of the slamming door reverberates in my ears. Instead of fading, it seems to get louder and louder until I plug my ears with my fingers to block it out. But it's inside my head—my world exploding around me.

My legs go limp, and I reach out to protect myself as I fall onto the floor. With my fingers out of my ears, I realize I'm making animal bleats, but I can't stop. A spasm in my stomach jerks me into a fetal curl and I see speckles in front of my eyes. Then all my senses overload in a flashing roar. I throw back my head and scream.

Chapter 13

Mom drives me to the loony bin Friday around noon.

She found me on the floor on Tuesday, after my argument with Geoff, and helped me to bed. I didn't get up the next day at all except to pee. Yesterday, she came into the bedroom and suggested again that I check into the hospital for a psych evaluation. I just nodded. Whatever. A bed would be available today.

Now she chatters out enough words for both of us.

"As an adult, you can't be locked up without your permission unless you are dangerous or break some laws. So you'll have to sign a form agreeing to this eval, as a voluntary patient."

I say nothing. I've barely spoken since my blow up. Nor have I kept track of my dreams. For all I know, I could be dreaming now. For example, I just saw Mom run a yellow light, and she doesn't do that normally.

I glance over at Mom without turning my head. She has white knuckles on the steering wheel. That seems real.

Her words whirl by my face so fast I can't tell if she's rambling or I'm unable to pay attention.

"This is just to be sure. That's all. Won't you feel better when schizophrenia is ruled out? You still fall in the onset age window, you know."

God, don't let me have schizophrenia. Most people who suffer from it don't lead happy lives. Even on meds they are severely disabled, and many hate taking them. I sure don't want to go there.

Unless I have to.

I let her voice bounce around in the car, full of reassurances, as active as I am passive. I already know what to expect. I've been through this routine before. I was younger then, and more willing to see my parents as wise.

At the hospital they will run a new sleep study on me along with physical and psych evals. But they may try me out on meds, which I dread. The meds are always horrible. I wish I could quit thinking about that part.

The best part about the mental wing is that I can let down my watchfulness—be myself—let the specialists see me at my worst. If I talk from my dreams, nobody gets hurt, including me. "A restful three-day stay," Mom called it, and that's partly true. A picture of Geoff pops into my head. I push it away. Who knows if we'd be in touch even if I was at home. In fact, it wouldn't be likely. I've never seen him so angry.

Mom and I climb out of the car together at the hospital. She plays with her hair and shuffles her feet. I must be moving slowly.

"Come on sweetie. I'll go in and get you settled for the weekend."

Mom hands me my backpack. I've brought clothes from home to wear. Thank goodness they let me dress normally. I also brought my journal, my cellphone with my calendar, some pens and my zombie novel. Wonder what the shrink will think about that?

I hope they let me keep my stuff. The first time, they locked everything away until I left. That was brutal. But the last time they didn't even look at what I brought. I hope they haven't changed their procedure since then.

The check-in process is quick. They have my file and my recent paperwork already. The registrar hands a card to Mom. "Incoming and outgoing calls are screened through the main desk and logged in the patient file. Here's a card with the extension."

Too soon, Mom says goodbye and hugs me. I try to hug back, but before I can get my arms to work, she has pulled away, her face seamed with worry. The security guard buzzes her out through the locked doors.

An orderly leads me to the ninth floor wing: the mental ward. He gives me the tour: TV room, cafeteria, laundry, bathroom with a real tub, landline wall phones, the hallway down which most of my meetings will take place, and my digs. My insurance only covers a semi-private room, so I meet my roommate. She's in her mid-twenties and looks heavily medicated. She has tried to put on makeup with an unsteady hand. The result is heavy and uneven.

As much as I feel I belong with the crazies, I also am revolted by the fact. I'm not similar to my roommate at all. But to be fair, I haven't spoken with her yet.

In my room is a locker where I can keep my backpack, and there are unlocked drawers for my clothes. I don't think I'll unpack. It's a brief stay. I don't want to feel too connected to this place. Especially if life is easier here than at home.

The orderly hands me a sheet with times and appointments on it. None are in my room; they all take place elsewhere. There's a map printed on the back so I can find where to go. My sleep study is tonight, in the regular side of the hospital. They probably scheduled it right away because they want to monitor my dreams before they give me any drugs. I roll my eyes.

"Questions?" The orderly must have seen my expression. I shake my head no and give him my dismissive smile.

"Oh, I almost forgot." His voice freezes my heart. "I need to put your cellphone away for safekeeping. No texting, e-mail or Internet connections are allowed without special permission, though there are two communal computers and a printer in the break room that you can use locally." He sticks out his hand.

In grim silence, I dig in my backpack and pull out my cellphone. He doesn't ask what else I have in there. I could have slipped in my iPad, which has its own wifi and phone link. I would have, had I'd thought of it. Another indication that my brain is screwy.

I hand the phone to the orderly, who pulls a manila envelope from behind the papers attached to his clipboard, writes my name and room number across the top, and drops the cell inside. He hands me a receipt that I put on the top shelf of my locker. I stash my backpack away, my journal inside it. I leave the appointment sheet on my bedside table. The orderly leaves and closes my door behind him. After a moment, I get up and open it again. I feel boxed in here.

"Whasup?" My roommate's voice is a slur. She swallows and tries again. "Why'd ya open the door? You afraid of me?" She gives a ghastly grin. I wonder if she thinks she's friendly.

"Hardly. The room's claustrophobic. I don't want to be here."

"Like, who does? I close the door 'cause the things sneak in. Ya know how they are." She shakes her head wisely. "I'm Luna. What's yer name?"

"Tiegen." In my head I start calling her Looney Luna.

"Whatcha in for?"

She sounds like I'm incarcerated. I consider answering, "Murder One," but decide that Luna's sense of humor may be blunted right now.

"I can't tell dreams from reality sometimes," I tell her, even though she's a stranger. In here, unlike home, I've no need to hide my problems. Everybody's messed up. And considering how altered her consciousness may be, she probably won't remember anyway.

"I hear ya," Luna says. "Sometimes I dream when I'm 'wake. Like when the voices start, 'n I'm sure they're in the room, ya know? The meds quiet 'em down, but I wanna sleep all the time and I don't have much fun. So I go off 'em 'n end up back in here all drugged up. That crap really gets to ya." She shakes her head slowly back and forth. The repetitive movement hypnotizes her, and her eyes glaze over as the motion gradually slows.

"Umm." I don't know what to say. I flop down on my bed. "What do people do here during the day?"

She blinks her eyes and wakes up a smidgeon. "I dunno. Group meetin's, craft projects, yoga, more groups, quiet time. Some take 15 minute walks outside, but not me. Ya gotta earn that."

"What do you do instead?"

Watch TV, I guess. There's news at 5. Dinner's at 5:30. Ya hungry?"

"Maybe I will be by then." The alarm clock by my bed tells me I have several hours free, so I get out my zombie mystery and settle in for a read.

"Whatcha readin'? Zombie stuff? Oh yeah. I saw a zombie once. It did somethin' to my brain. You can't trust 'em—zombies." She nods her head sagely.

Obviously, this isn't going to work. I pop the book closed and stand up. "Guess I'll explore. They told me to settle in, whatever that means. I'll close the door for you. Keep the things out." I walk out of the room and close the door before Luna can respond. I consider reading in the bath, but figure someone will want their turn the moment I get the temperature exactly right.

I wander down the grey hall, through the drab TV room with its bare walls, and find another nondescript room with several tables. The Occupational Therapy room. A jigsaw puzzle spreads across one table.

A guy and a girl sit in the room. The girl is in a wheelchair, staring straight ahead. The guy is rocking. I see the attraction of both these coping strategies, although I have other plans right now. But the two patients are quiet, and that's what I need. I draw a chair over to the window, put one foot up on a second chair and open my book.

* * *

By Saturday night, I've had a sleep-study, taken a bunch of tests, seen the analyst, gone to physical and occupational therapy (I'm not sure why), gotten a cheery call from Mom, and been given a shot of something from the psychiatrist that makes me dizzy. I shamble when I walk. Nice to fit in.

The shot is supposed to suppress my dreams tonight. I'd like it to work, but I haven't much hope. Drugs have always made life worse, because I'm altered as well as wacko. I can't imagine why Geoff would choose to feel this.

Besides, from what I've read, if you don't dream, it screws up your waking mind. We need dreams in order to be healthy. Even if, as in my case, having dreams may not be particularly helpful in other ways.

Loony Luna snores in the next bed. I change into my pajamas, climb into bed and wait for sleep. Strange thoughts dart through my head, and I can't chase them away. Nor can

I concentrate on the zombies until I'm sober again. So I think about my recent favorite topic instead.

I wonder what Geoff is doing. I wish he were here to snuggle up against—I know I'd sleep better. I wonder if he went to the gym? Probably dumped all that when he dumped me. That's for the best. At least he's safe from Flex.

That line of thinking does not help me sleep. I force a yawn, roll over on the hard mattress in my single bed, and blank my mind. The plastic covering, to protect the mattress from bodily fluids, crunches under the sheets every time I move. How special. Monday I go home to my own bed—a good mantra. I begin to chant silently. *I can make it till Monday.*

Honestly, I can't wait.

* * *

Sunday evening, before dinner, I hit the TV room for the five o'clock news. The top story is from last night—a bizarre, burning cross was erected in some guy's front yard. One neighbor, and then another, are interviewed by a news reporter. Sounds like they had a spontaneous block party in front of the victim's house with everyone oohing and ah-ing at the flames. Great entertainment.

"The occupant of the house was not home when the fire was set," the reporter says. "The cross had burned down to coals by the time he returned a moment ago. I'm awaiting a statement. Here: he's on his way over."

"No." The homeowner speaks into the microphone, "I have no enemies. It must have been a joke. Or inadequately supervised kids." He doesn't seem too bothered by the whole thing.

But when they zoom in on the man's face, I'm pretty sure it's the dark-haired fellow I saw leaving the gym—the one I suspected was a target of Flexman's ire. If true, then cross-burning may be the "something small" that Flexman promised before he "really teaches them."

The more I think about this, the surer I am that it's true. I've got to let someone know right away. Jessica St. Marie must hear about this tonight!

I walk down the hall to the wall phones, all of which are in use. I sit and wait, drumming my fingers on my knees. It takes ages before I get my turn. I dial the extension for the main desk, and ask to be connected to the Police Station. The person at the other end pauses while he notes my name and who I'm calling. I begin to wonder if he'll tell my call is off-limits, but then the phone rings.

First, a recording tells me to dial 911 if this is an emergency. Then someone answers, "Police Station."

"Officer St. Marie, please."

"I'm afraid she doesn't work weekends. Can another officer assist you?"

I think about it, but it seems too difficult to explain everything.

"Ma'am? Are you still there?"

"No thanks. I'll try Monday."

I hang up, and another patient pushes past me for a turn at the phone. My anger sparks, but I get back in line, muttering.

When it is my turn again, I call Geoff on James' landline. Only he and I know what's going on. Even if we're on the outs, someone needs to stop Flexman from hurting anyone.

James' mother answers the phone and I ask for Geoff.

"Hello?" It's his voice, and my heart flutters. I clear my throat.

"Hi Geoff. It's Tiegen."

"We're done, Tiegen. Don't call again." He hangs up.

Before another patient can take my place, I redial his number. Again, I get James' mother.

"Sorry, I got cut off. May I speak to Geoff again, please?"

A few moments later I hear someone pick up the phone and then hang it up. He didn't speak. I hang up and walk back to the break room.

My head snaps from side to side as I look around. Of course, the computer is useless without a wifi connection, and nobody has a cell I can borrow. We're together in the wacko ward. No wifi. I kick myself for not slipping my iPad into my backpack.

I put my head in my hands. I'm in a prison of my own choice.

I'm trapped.

Chapter 14

I get up and walk to the nurse's station. "Excuse me." I use my ultra-polite voice.

"Yes?" A nurse glances up at me then back to her paperwork.

"I need to send an e-mail, please. Just a quick one. To tell a friend to be sure and watch the news tonight." I give my sweet, hopeful smile, the one that makes people do things for me.

With a sigh, the nurse pulls out my chart and opens it. "You are not allowed e-mail privileges." She marks the information with her index finger. She doesn't look up at my smile.

"How about if you e-mail the message for me?" I try my smile again. "That wouldn't break the rules."

"If your doctor okays it, I'd be glad to." She glances up just as my smile mutates.

I consider my few options. I could call Mom and beg her to let James' Mom know that I want Geoff to tune in to the news. But I know I'll be bombed with unwanted questions. Plus, like the childhood game of telephone, that line of communication is bound to break down somewhere along the line.

Then I remember that on Sunday evenings Mom and Dad go out for a movie and dinner. They never get back before 8:00 p.m. I've got a long wait before I can call them.

I am still standing at the nurse's station, though I notice that the nurse has gone back to her computer, ignoring my presence. I clear my throat to get her attention.

"Is my doctor here tonight? I could check with her now about that message for my friend."

"Left at 5:00. You just missed her."

"Please, just send my friend that quick e-mail, won't you? Just say, 'Tiegen wants you to watch tonight's 11:00 news.' That would be such a help. I know my doctor wouldn't mind. I'm self-admitted, you know."

"Not without your doctor's written permission." Her voice shifts from firm to stern.

I'm obviously making no friends here. "Thank you anyway." I give the smile one more time. Then I walk away from the desk before she logs me as a trouble maker. I wait to grumble until I'm out of her earshot.

I stalk into my room. My roommate is sitting on her bed, her hands clutched in her lap like a little girl in trouble at school.

"Hey Luna. I need to get a message out of here tonight, and there's no Internet. Do you know of any way I can do that?"

"Use the phone."

"I tried that."

"Ask the angels then."

"Who are they?"

She presses her lips together and scowls at me. "What are you, stupid? You know. Angel angels. Like, with wings." Her condescending voice rises at the end as if she'd asked a question. She lets go of her hands and makes flapping motions from the shoulders before returning her locked fingers to her lap.

"Right. The angels. But I have to tell my friend to watch the 11:00 news," I say. "You know angels, sometimes they have other priorities. This is time sensitive, and really important."

"You could ask the orderly who works nights here. He'd prolly do it for a little tail. It's happened before."

I shudder. "I'd rather not go that far."

"Then it's not all that important, is it? I mean really?" Luna rolls her eyes.

"I guess not." No help here. But as I think about her suggestion, I remember that I shoved a twenty-dollar bill into my backpack. I could try paying a staff member to deliver my message.

I get my backpack out of the locker, and open the front pocket to take out the money. It was folded in half the short way, then in half again the long way so that it would be easy to hide if I wasn't allowed to keep it. I see it right away, but as I reach in, my finger catches in the pocket's lining. It appears to be coming loose from the pocket itself.

I look closer, pull on it, and see a gap in the lining at the seam. I stick three fingers into the hole and feel a piece of paper inside. I pull out the list that I picked up at the library—the one I couldn't find for Jessica St. Marie. Folded in half, it is only a quarter sheet—anything larger wouldn't have fit.

A tingle runs through my body as I realize what this means. My breath comes faster. My eyes grow wide.

Now I have a double reason to get in touch with Geoff. Not only must he hear about the cross burning incident on the news, but I need to let him know I found this piece of paper—that I'm not crazy. That I can prove that the guy on the TV may be in danger.

I have to let Jessica know as well. When I last talked to her, she was really upset with us for following Flexman. If anything, I think it made her less likely to believe anything I told her.

I think about this for a minute, weighing its importance. After all, I get out tomorrow after lunch if I do nothing. But by then Geoff will miss the news, and Jessica won't be alerted to its significance. That's plenty of time for Flexman to go after the second guy, or to pull off a more dangerous crime. Now that I have found the proof, I know she'll take this seriously.

I stick both the twenty and the paper into my pocket, and go walk the halls. Perhaps the solution will come to me. Maybe I can locate an employee who will help me out. At least, there's a better chance I'll get my message out than if I stay in my room, talking with Luna and the angels.

The rooms that make up the mental health wing are all familiar now, and the space doesn't seem as big as it did on Friday. On my second circle around the area the nurse I spoke to earlier looks up at me.

"Are you okay?"

"Fine. I'm fine."

"You are pacing the halls."

I think quickly. "No, just getting some exercise. Walking laps so I'll sleep better." I nod at her and move on quickly. Then I change my circuit so that I avoid her station, but I continue to pace until dinner time.

* * *

During dinner, I see that a night orderly has come on shift. He's a plain-looking fellow, balding, in his 40's with acne scars and a big nose. I watch him when I think he won't notice. Would he be the type who might get the information to Geoff for me or would he be a stickler for the rules? He wears no rings—might be a loner who appreciates company. That encourages me a bit.

By the time dinner ends, no other man has appeared. The orderly may be my only choice. I'm not worried about wasting my twenty dollars, but I'm not interested in sex with this guy, if that is the going rate as Luna seems to indicate.

I also don't want to get in trouble, as that might make me look crazier than I am. I want clear results from my tests—that's why I checked myself in—and I don't want to be given any more meds. Once last night's dose wore off, I decided not to take anything else. I hate feeling logy. I may not know what I need, but what I don't need is easy—psychotropic meds. No more.

My best chance to catch the orderly's attention may be as he leaves the dining room. The patients have all left by now except the frozen girl in the wheelchair and me.

I turn in my tray to the bussing area, and wait in the corridor outside the cafeteria. I bend down to retie one shoe, then the other, a favorite geocaching ploy when people are about. I untie them and tie them again. Then I wonder if I should wait somewhere else. After all, there must be other doors he can use to leave the cafeteria, since he's staff.

I go to the TV room and take a seat where I can watch either the TV or the door to the cafeteria, which is now closed. I can also see who comes down two hallways. A far superior viewpoint. I half-watch the TV and wait.

Fifteen minutes go by, before I spot the orderly. He walks towards me down one of the halls. I was right about there being another exit from the cafeteria. Good thing I didn't wait any longer out by the cafeteria door.

I get up and amble in his direction, making sure I stop him before he gets too close to the TV room, which is full of patients. I'd rather not have anyone see us together. When I stop him, I ask, in a soft voice, if I can talk to him alone for a minute. I give him what I hope is my intriguing smile — not too suggestive — one that will make him curious about what I have to say.

He agrees, and we walk back down the hall the way he came. Then he stops and asks how he can help. I explain about my e-mail message.

"I can't do that without your doctor's permission."

"I know the rule, but this isn't a personal message, nothing about a relationship or the hospital or anything. I just want to tell him two things — that he should watch tonight's news, and to contact a police officer about a paper she wanted. That's it."

"It's still not allowed. Plus, all email out is subject to review. If there was trouble, somebody would identify it as coming from my account, and I'd be fired."

"I can create a fake gmail address and e-mail it from there," I suggest. "That way, if anyone did notice it, they wouldn't know who sent it. The most they could do is guess that it came from me, because I knew the recipient."

"I don't think it's a good idea." He sounds less sure than he did before. I press my advantage.

"I have twenty bucks I'd give you as a thank you."

"That doesn't change the rules."

"No, but it makes it more worth your while, right?"

He looks me over, as if unsure what to do. I can tell he's wavering, though.

"I could throw in a kiss." I give him a wink. Then I wonder where that came from. Maybe insanity is contagious.

He glances around, and seeing nobody, takes out a bunch of keys and heads toward an unmarked door.

"Come in here. This computer is for staff use. Let's do it quickly." He opens the door and gestures me in, looking up and down the hall again. As soon as we're inside, he locks the door.

"I'll set up the gmail account. It only takes a minute."

He gestures to the keyboard, and I sit down and click the browser while he watches over my shoulder. I set up a gmail account called Flexman, open an e-mail window and write my quick message. I add Geoff's e-mail address, and hit send before the guy can change his mind.

"Hey, did you send that already? What about my money?"

I stand up and back toward the door as I extend my hand holding the twenty. "It's right here. I appreciate your help." I smile my dismissive smile and scrabble for the knob behind me with my other hand, but it doesn't work. He has turned the bolt on the door. Now he covers it with his hand and leans his weight casually against that arm.

"And my kiss?" He leers at me, and steps into my interpersonal space.

All my senses tell me to turn and run, but if he keeps to his part of the bargain, I don't want to make waves. I take a deep breath and lean my face towards him from where I stand a step away.

But he doesn't kiss me until he grabs me, sticks his hands down the back of my pants, and pulls me up against his groin. He sticks his tongue so far into my mouth that I have to fight my gag impulse. The moment he relaxes his hold I say, "There you go, we're even. We better get out of here before we get caught."

He has other ideas. He kisses me again, and squeezes my buttocks with one hand while he moves the other to his zipper. Seems my roommate's brain isn't pickled after all. This time, when he pauses for breath, I twist away and say, "You got more than we bargained for. Now let me out of here before I scream for help."

He stands looking at me, panting a little, his fly half undone, obviously amazed that I wouldn't want more of him.

I open my mouth wide and take a deep breath.

Disgust paints his face. "Stay inside until I tell you it's okay."

I nod, and he opens the door and steps outside. Then he pokes his head in, "It's clear."

As I pass, he murmurs. "I work tomorrow, too…"

Like I care.

I walk quickly back to the TV room while he locks the door. There is safety in numbers.

When I haven't seen him for a while, I return to my room, where Luna sits just as she did before dinner. I wonder if she remembered to eat.

I rinse out my mouth in the sink. Then I brush my teeth. Luna still hasn't moved.

"I've got another question," I dry my face. "What happens if you leave here before your three days are up?" She turns her head to me. Comprehension flashes in her eyes.

"Ya get busted. They chart that ya left Against Medical Advice, and they get the police to throw ya back in here." I can hear the capital letters in her emphasis. "Then they drug ya so ya don't do it again. I know, I've tried."

"But I checked myself in. Can't I leave if I need to?"

"Dunno. Never checked myself in. Why would ya do that?"

"Long story."

"Well, ya'd still be AMA. Could screw things up."

She's probably right. My insurance might not cover this weekend, and finances are tight. But standing here, I realize that Geoff might not read his e-mail tonight. Or my message might get caught in his spam filter.

What if Flex acts out tonight? Do I just ignore what I know and let him injure someone? A grim thought.

Sending the message just isn't enough. It might be no better than bargaining with the angels. I need to reach the police right away. And there's no way I can do it right except in person, with my guarantee of sanity in hand. Even if it messes up my eval results. Even with an AMA on my record.

I open my locker and grab my backpack, stuffing the few items I've taken out back inside. I make sure my pajamas and toothbrush are on top of my other stuff. Then I take my green appointment sheet and fold it so the days of the week don't show. I circle the cell that says, "Sleep Study," throw the pack up on one shoulder, and head for the door out of my room.

"Whatcha doin' now?" Luna seems a little too interested.

"I've got a second sleep study tonight. I thought of skipping it, but it's probably easier to go." I roll my eyes and shrug before stepping out the door.

Remembering the route that I took Friday night, I walk toward the exit door from the unit, I wave my green sheet at the guard and say, "Sleep study again. I couldn't sleep on Friday, so we're going to try tonight." I zip open the top of my pack so he can see my pjs.

He smiles and clicks the door lock. I walk through. Until I'm sure I'm out of his sight, I stroll down the corridor I walked on Friday night. Then I start looking for indications of elevators or an exit. Coming around a corner, I see a stairway, so I clamber down two flights. I see a nurse's station.

"Excuse me, I'm turned around. Can you remind me how to get to the front door?"

The nurse smiles, as if used to helping the lost, and gives me directions.

Without incident, I find my way out. The air tastes sweet.

Then I realize I have no car, no bike, and no money left for a cab. My folk's house and Geoff's are about three miles away and the police station is only a little closer, but mostly in the opposite direction. Somehow, I didn't think this far when planning my escape. But having no other choice, I slip both straps of my backpack onto my arms, and then shrug it onto my shoulders.

I walk.

Chapter 15

The first half mile of my walk is the same whether I head to the police station, near the library, or to Geoff's. I use that time to consider my options. Chances are, nobody will notice I'm gone from the hospital until lights-out at 10:00 pm or even early morning, if they believe Luna about the second sleep study. If I'm really lucky, I might get back before the uproar.

I can't go home—my mother would explode if she knew I had walked off the psycho ward after finally agreeing to check myself in. She'd want to talk it all through, and the time to act would be gone.

The Police Station? While someone is always available at the P.D., Jessica St. Marie isn't there. Starting over alone with my initial report, a TV news story, and a new officer doesn't appeal to me. At least not alone.

I want Geoff along, if he'll come. He's been my conscience on this since the beginning. He'll keep me straight if I mess up the story. I really screwed up when I drove him away. I've got to apologize even if he never sees me again. Maybe we can brainstorm a way to get to the P.D. together without a car. I'd appreciate a second brain sifting through my plans. But will he speak to me? There's no way to tell.

It's about 7:00 pm, so I have about two and a half hours before dark. The late nights this far north are a boon during the summer.

At the turning point, I gulp down my fears about our fight and turn toward Geoff's house.

* * *

James and Geoff live in a rambler, which helps when one is hiding out. On TV, actors always throw a pebble at the upstairs window to get someone's attention. I've wondered how they aim so accurately. Why doesn't anyone ever hear the clink, besides the correct person? Don't they ever hit the wrong window? And how do they keep from cracking the glass? With my recent bad luck, I'd probably crash it right through the pane and bring the whole family running.

But with this rambler, I can walk around the side, directly to Geoff's window. Nobody is inside, but I tap lightly on the glass anyway. No answer. This early in the evening though, he might be eating dinner or watching TV.

I circle the house, peeking into windows, trying to find Geoff without being seen. He isn't in the TV room where James is mindlessly eating ice cream straight from the carton, his eyes glued to the screen.

The living room windows, I leave until last. There's not much cover between me and those inside, or between the windows and the street. I am exposed from all directions.

I crouch down low between a small bush and the house. Moving slowly, I peer just over the sill.

The living room, dining room and kitchen are one large open space with white walls and deep carpet. Sure enough, Geoff sits at the dining table, no longer eating, but talking with James' dad and fiddling with his fork.

Unfortunately, Geoff's back faces me while James' dad sits side-on to the window, and I can think of no way of getting Geoff to look at me without drawing unwanted attention. I make myself as small as possible, and inch my head up just high enough to check the room every couple of minutes.

Finally, Geoff gets up and stretches, and then leaves. It looks like he may go back to his bedroom, so I scurry over there as quickly as I can without being noticed. This time, when I tap at his window, he comes over.

Darting a quick look over his shoulder, he opens the window.

"What are you doing here? You're supposed to be locked in the hospital. And in case you didn't understand when I hung up the phone, it's over—I don't want to talk to you." His voice is a hiss.

"I'm AWOL, because something has happened. Have you read your e-mail tonight? Or checked out the local news?"

He shakes his head no, and I fill him in: the cross-burning, Flexman's note, and my escape from the hospital. He listens without comment until I pause. Then he sighs.

"Look. I got caught up in that Flexman rubbish because it was important to you, even though it made me nervy. When it looked dangerous, I wanted to protect you. But I'm not sure I want anything to do with it anymore. My tenure as novice detective is over. And you shouldn't have come here."

"I'm truly sorry about our fight. I said some really stupid stuff. I should have known better than to suspect you. You've always been good to me.

"But I've got to get to the police station and show them the note right away, before Flex does something worse, and I want you to come along. The guy with the cross in his yard on TV was the one I glimpsed at the gym the other day. The burning happened around this time yesterday. Flexman could take action against the other guy tonight."

"Or take that more drastic step with the first guy that he alluded to at the library." His voice is slow, but I can tell he gets the potential seriousness of Flexman's actions. My knees wobble as I realize he still might believe me. I put down my pack and pull out the elusive note of Flexman's.

"That's what I'm afraid of. It's the main reason I made my breakout. Burnt crosses make me think of the Ku Klux Klan, but I think that's a distraction. Flex's got something else planned. Look, here's the note I told you about and then promptly lost. Look at it."

Geoff examines the note and catches his breath. "Is there any way to get your bicycle out of your garage? If so, we can tackle the police issue together."

I take back the note and carefully tuck it back deep inside.

"My folks should be away at the movies, so yeah, I can grab the bike. I'll get it right now and come back, so the neighbors won't see us together."

Geoff nods, then closes his window and goes to tell someone that he's off for a ride on James' bike. I hurry home.

When he catches up with me at my place, we ride up the street, away from people who know me. Then we glide around a block and head downtown.

At the P.D., we lock our bikes and ask the receptionist if we can speak to a police officer. We are directed to Officer

Peter Landsbury. He pulls up my initial report, makes a photocopy of the paper with Flexman's notes on it, and writes down the additional information we share. We tell him about everything except my dreams and my escape from the hospital this evening.

"The connection is weak, but you make a good case. And you believe that this man is likely to commit another hate crime soon?"

"I do. I'm so sure of it, I couldn't wait until tomorrow to see Jennifer. Someone needs to follow up on this tonight, or the two Muslim men may get hurt. Since Flexman got away with a cross burning last night, he's probably confident that he can move forward without being caught."

Peter looks from one of us to the other. "I don't like the way you two played cops. That was dangerous and, by our rules, premature. This is work for professionals."

We utter the apologies he seems to want to hear, and admit that he is right about the risk. I nod my head and try to look shamefaced. This is not the time to tell him how hard I've tried to hand this case over to the police. Then he seems to come to a decision.

"I'm going to call Officer St. Marie, and then I'll get back to you. Wait here."

While he's gone, Geoff and I sit quietly, all our words used up for the moment. Our eyes meet, and I give him a little apologetic smile. Geoff reaches over and squeezes my hand. There's a stubborn hope in his eyes. I wonder what he sees in mine.

"I'm sorry, Geoff. What I accused you of was awful. I promise to give you the benefit of the doubt if we're ever in that situation again. As soon as you asked if it was a dream, I realized I'd messed up. But my dreams aren't going away. I have to depend on the people around me to help when I mix things up. And you are one of the sweetest."

I hold my breath for his reply. After a pause, he answers.

"I was determined not to, but I missed you, Tiegen. I hate the accusations you made, especially that I'd run around on you. That seemed like the end of us. But then, without you, I realized how much I enjoyed our outings—even our detective work. It may take time to trust you again, but I'm willing to try."

I lean toward him, and he gives me a brief kiss on the lips.

Peter Landsbury reappears saying, "Officer St Marie verified all you said. She's glad that you found the paper with the notes. She had feared you were pranking us—that the information was a fabrication. Now, though, she agrees that the cross burning is the connection that makes your concerns valid. She convinced me to take you seriously."

I exhale sharply, not realizing how much I'd been depending on his next words. "So you'll check the guy out?"

"Yes. But we need to quit calling him Flexman and search out his real name. I also need to check if he has priors. You'll have to excuse me again." And he leaves.

Geoff and I play with each other's fingers. When our eyes meet, it feels like it did before our fight.

This time, Peter is gone for longer, though probably fewer than 10 minutes. His eyes are wide and his movements quick when he returns.

"I just got a call. There's been a second incident."

Chapter 16

We climb into Peter Landsbury's police cruiser, and with the siren blaring, we speed to an unfamiliar residential neighborhood on the edge of town. Peter makes us promise to stay in the car while he goes to the front door, but he wants to know if either of us can identify the victim.

On the grass, a chunk of wood burns into embers. Seems that it was another cross. Peter returns, accompanied by someone from the house.

Geoff catches his breath.

"You recognize him?"

"That's the other chap from the gym."

We watch as Peter fills out a crime report and takes photos. Neighbors have gathered, and he sets out crime scene ribbon, blocking the property before footprints or other evidence is obliterated. He makes several calls on his cell phone before returning to us in the cruiser.

"Well, is that him?" Peter asks Geoff.

"That's the chap. He was also at the gym."

"I thought you'd say that." Peter takes off his hat and scratches his head. "I'm the reporting officer, so I need to stay here until Detective Johanson or the Criminalist arrives. Sorry, but you'll have to wait with me for a bit.

We agree, but as the wood burns low, I realize how late it's getting. Shadows creep out from their hiding places and stretch across the yard.

Still we wait.

I reach for my cell phone to check the time, then remember that it is in a manila envelope at the hospital.

"Geoff, what time is it?

He pulls out his cell. "Nine forty-five."

We look at each other. I'm not going to make it back to the hospital before lights out. I may not even be free much longer. If Luna is right, the next call Peter answers may be the hospital telling him to pick up an escaped mental patient—who conveniently sits in his back seat.

The darkness deepens. I've run out of time. Though it's too late to get back to the hospital, I also don't dare go back to my folks' house, because they might try to keep me from seeing this investigation through. I don't dare sleep at Geoff's house, as that will be the first place my parents call once they are informed I've gone AMA. And I don't want to put such pressure on our bond when we've just gotten back together. Plus, there's no reason we both have to get in trouble. I wonder what it would be like to sleep on the streets like a homeless person tonight.

Nights at the psych ward suddenly seem warm and safe in comparison, even with Luna snoring in the bed next to mine.

I swallow hard.

* * *

When Geoff and I leave the police station, it's after 11:00 pm. We've argued with Peter Landsbury for nearly an hour. I am exhausted.

The issue with Flexman (whose real name is Syd Douglas) seems so simple to me: arrest the guy before he hurts someone! But by police rules, it is too early to take that step.

Peter told us, "There has to be physical evidence—like scraps of wood left over from constructing the crosses in Douglas' possession. The connections you two outlined will not stand up in court. They're circumstantial. But you've been very helpful. Douglas is firmly on our suspect list."

In fact, he and Baldy are the only people on the suspect list. And Geoff and I have been warned not to get in the way of the investigation from here on out. So now we stand outside the Police Department in the dark, our bikes in their racks, my spirits in the depths.

"Was all our work for nothing?" I scuff my toe in the dirt illuminated by the precinct's lighting.

"Of course not," he says, but goes quiet instead of supporting his point of view.

"Do you really believe that the police will follow up, and get the evidence to arrest them?"

"Maybe."

"Well, I worry that they won't do much until Flexman, uh Douglas, has already hurt someone. That's no good. That's what I've been trying to avoid all along."

"I know. Me too." Geoff shrugs and lifts his hands in what looks like surrender.

But I'm not ready to surrender. Not after I predicted some action on Douglas' part, and then he burned those crosses. The police need to take decisive action to stop him right away.

My mind spins, too burned out to find a solution. I need sleep so I can think more clearly in the morning.

Peter never mentioned my escape from the psych ward, so the cops mustn't know. Maybe nobody cares if a self-admitted adult walks out. But there's an outside chance that the hospital staff believed Luna about the redo of my sleep study. If so, maybe I can sneak back, early tomorrow. It's a better chance than trying to return more than an hour past lights out.

If only I had money for a motel room. I remember giving my twenty dollars to the slimy hospital orderly. It wouldn't have been enough, anyway. I need my charge card, and it's at home in my wallet. My parents will be home by now, so it's too late to get it. I should have grabbed it when I got my bike. No way will I ask Geoff for that much money. I want things to go smoothly with him for a while. We'd argue when he asked what the money was for.

I decide.

"Hey Geoff, may I see your cell phone for a minute?"

"Sure." He hands it to me and raises his eyebrows in a question mark.

"I need to check my e-mail and make a call or two." I study the phone so I don't see his face. Angling myself so he can't read the screen, I pull up my geocaching account.

Many geocaches hide in greenbelts around town. When I search for them, I often see evidence that homeless people have slept under the trees among the native salal and ferns. It's very common, so it must be reasonably safe. I've never heard of violence against local homeless where they sleep. Sleeping outside might be like camping out when I was a kid. Not so bad.

As I skim though the list of caches I've visited, I realize that the closest one is right behind the Woodsdale Recreation Center. The library, the rec center and the P.D. are all located in a row along 44th Ave. But behind them lies an area large enough to hide a sleeper. Or several.

Geoff will never go for me sleeping outside, and I won't risk another fight. So I dial my cell number and imagine it ringing inside its manila envelope at the ward. I pretend I hear an answer on the other end.

"Hi, Amanda. Sorry to call so late." I pause as if listening. "Oh, that's cool. Hey, can I crash on your couch tonight?" I pause again. "Sweet, woman. I'll be right over. Thanks."

"I found a place to sleep tonight," I lie. "With a friend who lives a few blocks away. You can walk me to her house before you ride home. I'll meet you back here in the morning, and we can see where Flex, I mean Douglas, goes before I return to the hospital."

"Come home with me and sleep at James' place. I'll take care of you. I can even sneak you breakfast." A slight smile flickers in the corners of his mouth. Does he think I've set this up to get an invite?

I'm enticed, but Geoff's place is terribly obvious. "That's the first place my folks will call when they hear I left the ward. They'll tell James' parents, and then we'll both in trouble. We may lose our freedom to make sure that the police cover Douglas tomorrow.

"Really, Amanda's is fine. It will be fun to catch up with her before we go to sleep. All you and I need is a time to meet back by my bike at the P.D. in the morning."

Geoff scowls, but agrees. He unchains his bike and walks it and me to a house a few blocks away that I point out to him. I choose one with lights on inside.

"See? She has the porchlight on for me. Now go. She doesn't need to see us together, or get tangled up in all this. Better if all she knows is that I need a place to crash."

Geoff gazes into my eyes for a long moment. Then he forms his lips to mine, and a tingle runs down to my toes.

"Please, Tiegen. Come back with me and wait outside my window. As soon as everyone's asleep, I'll let you crawl inside and into my bed. Nobody comes into my room after I've retired. They respect my privacy."

I hear his British short "i" in the word, but for once, it doesn't make me smile. Inside of me, a battle rages, and I fight on both sides. I want to go with Geoff, and I want to be far from him if I'm found out. He kisses me again.

"I'll have my cellphone beep us before anyone else gets up—I know their habits. Then you can slip back outside," he says. "James' folks won't see you."

"Doesn't sound like enough hours of sleep," I say, weakening.

"And you really think you're going to get more here?"

No, I certainly don't, but I won't say so.

"If I let you win this argument, we put so much more on the line, Geoff."

I realize I'm not just talking about being caught by my folks.

"Not true. You are important to me. I love you."

And of course, that clinches it. How could I say no again?

* * *

I wake up in bed with Geoff, glad I let him convince me to stay at his place after all. His arm lies thrown across me, and I feel safe. Did I actually consider sleeping in a park? This is so much better. I pull my t-shirt to straighten it where it's become twisted. Wearing my underwear on the bottom, my legs are much more comfortable. His skin touches mine.

A pre-dawn riot of birdsong sounds outside the window. That's probably what woke me up. Inside is silent except for Geoff's soft breathing beside me. I think I can doze a trifle longer. His family's unlikely to be up at dawn.

I close my eyes again and remember his kisses, long and slow and dreamy. This night has been a slice of heaven. I've known Geoff such a short time, and already he says he loves me. I can't believe my luck.

Geoff mumbles something, half awake and half asleep, and pulls me toward him. I spoon up against his body, and rub one leg gently against his.

"Mmm," I say, and he kisses the back of my neck. This so beats lock-up in the hospital. It was worth breaking out, even with the mess I've created. But I don't need to think about that now. Life will collapse in on me all too soon.

For now, I snuggle up with a tiny moan of joy, and allow myself to doze.

* * *

The next time I awaken, my eyes still closed, I'm still cuddled up in Geoff's bed, warm and happy. His body should be pressed against my back. Only, it's a little too cool.

I roll back, expecting to feel Geoff's body at any moment. Instead I end up on my back on the cold ground, with nature poking in where my shirt has pulled free from the waistband of my pants.

I open my eyes to see a lanky man, dressed in mismatched, dirty clothing, who sits about twenty feet away, drinking a paper cup of coffee. I gasp and he turns toward me, his grin showing teeth rotted like some movie horror.

When he steps closer, I smell him: body odor, long unwashed clothes, urine, stale food, and smoky halitosis. I throw off my makeshift covers and jump up into a sprinter's crouch. I'd rather run than fight him, even as decrepit as he looks.

"Stop right there!" I yell.

I rise up on my toes, take a deep breath, and prepare to run.

Chapter 17

The homeless man sets down his coffee and holds both hands out, palms toward me. He steps back a couple of steps.

"Don't be afraid. I came across you a couple of hours ago, and I figured you were new on the streets. I watched you sleep — to make sure you got through the night safely.

"Thanks. It seems I'm fine." I straighten a bit, but remain ready to dash off. I flash on the hospital orderly, his tongue licking my uvula. I shudder.

But this guy is, well, just a nice guy. He offers to share his coffee with me, and it smells so good I almost give in. But looking at his teeth, I change my mind. To my shame, I'm fairly sure he reads my body language. He directs me where to go for my own cup.

"Just 79 cents."

"That's okay. I don't have any money. But my boyfriend is meeting me here soon, and he'll buy me something, I'm sure."

At that, the man turns out his pockets, finding a variety of odds and ends that he prods, turns over, then returns to their storage spots, though some would probably have been better thrown out. Then he takes off a ragged shoe and pokes around inside until he finds a foot-dampened, rumpled dollar bill. He hands it to me. It reeks.

"Get a cup while you wait." His voice is kind. "I know the streets. Coffee helps sharpen you up after you've slept outdoors. Bet you didn't sleep much."

"You're right." I take the dollar. Then I stuff everything back into my pack. "Thanks for looking out for me."

"Some of us have been around awhile. We're a community of sorts—keep track of each other. A couple of pimps search this area looking for runaways for the sex trade. They play on your insecurities, then act like your shining knight. Many get caught before we can warn them to get back home. It was the least I could do for you."

"I appreciate it. And I fully expect to be home by the end of the day." I give him a wave, realizing as I do so that I'm duplicating the wave Geoff usually gives to me. As I head off to find out what a 79 cent cup of fast-food coffee tastes like, I'm a little sorry that I won't see the man again.

But I have plenty to ponder. Two realities clash in my mind, and I have to get straight what really happened last night. I think back to where I stood in the street by my make-believe friend Amanda's house, and remember Geoff's kiss.

* * *

"Tell you what. I'll meet you back here at Amanda's in the morning, and we'll walk to the P.D. for your bike. I won't take any chance of something happening to you between here and there."

"Okay. Just wait until I come out before you show yourself."

"It's a deal." He kisses me again, sighs, and hops up on his bike. I wave as he pedals off down the street, and he waves back at the corner, before vanishing from sight.

Then I tromp back to the greenbelt, yawning, my eyelids half-closed.

I tense up before taking my first step between the trees. Spying nobody around, I tiptoe deeper into the greenbelt. Night turns the woods sinister, and my stomach screams that I should have gone to Geoff's. I convince myself that I can bike to his place, later, if I need to.

The cache I found is still hidden in its clever place, under a small bridge. I delay, turning it in my hands, while I listen for other people nearby. If someone comes up to me, I plan to yell and sprint toward the P.D. But nobody else is here.

From the discarded clothing and trash on the ground, I know I'm not the first to bed down in this mini-forest. I can find an unexposed pocket to slip inside.

After a short search, I choose a spot where several trees create a bower, backed up against a tall hedge of blackberry bushes with thorns that nobody would want to tackle. It can guard my back. My nest looks reasonably safe for a warm summer night — at least, safer than anywhere else I inspected. A patch of soft ground lies just beyond the blackberries.

My nerves calm, though my hands still shake as I dig through my backpack. *It's just a new experience*, I tell myself. I have two changes of clothes, so I put a black t-shirt over my white one, spread my pajamas under me, put the other clothes over me and use the backpack as a pillow.

Once I stretch out on my makeshift bed, my rebel eyes pop wide. I'm not an on-my-back sleeper, but if I roll onto my side, my hip grinds into the ground. I force my eyes closed. Hours pass, and scary thoughts jump into my mind each time I hear a rustle in the bushes. A tree leaf falls on my face, and I shriek before I realize that it is harmless. A stick cracks, and I hold my breath, waiting for an animal to charge me. *In the middle of Woodsdale? Get it together, Tieg.*

Somehow, I finally fall asleep.

* * *

I think about my journal, and how completely the dream with Geoff imitated reality. But I'm fairly certain that this time, the more dramatic story is truth. The homeless man was real, and not the snuggle in Geoff's bed. I want to write it all down, but other responsibilities weigh on me right now. I'll do it later.

At the burger joint, carrying my cheap cup of coffee, I go into the bathroom. I brush my hair and teeth, and put on the freshest looking of my clothes for the day. I even have fresh underwear I'd brought to wear at the hospital this morning which, more than anything else, make me feel ready for the day. I twist a couple of bizarre faces in the mirror. It's fun to see the mirror me look wacky for a change. Me? I'll do.

I take my coffee out to a table and sip it as the clock approaches 7:15 am, when I'll go back to the house where I last saw Geoff. By the time I toss my cup in the waste can and set out, I feel warm, awake, and ready to face my day.

At our meeting place, I grin. I've arrived before Geoff, as planned. Now he won't know that I slept outside. He'd only worry about me, and I don't want another argument.

"Good morning, my beauty," Geoff calls out as he skids to a stop next to me on his bike. "The night was long without you."

"It was. I didn't sleep nearly enough. But I had a lot of time to think about Douglas and how the police will deal with the cross burning incidents. I'm afraid they'll be too slow—that he'll commit more dangerous devilry before he's stopped."

"I agree. The crosses prove that you were right all along."

"Let's see where he goes when he leaves the gym. That could tell us a lot."

"After all the promises we made to Peter Landsbury last night, I feel weird about it, but I have no better plan. Let's stay invisible, though, okay?"

I nod, though I hardly need to be reminded.

We pick up my bike from the P.D., ride to the gym, and stake it out. We leave our bikes behind a pick-up that is parked in the lot across the street. I pull out a couple of wrinkled garments and fold them into cushions for us to sit on near our bikes. Making do is becoming a habit for me. Maybe I can work it into my dissertation somehow.

The view is clear, and as long as nobody chases us away, we will hang here for the long haul. There sure is a lot of waiting and watching involved in being an amateur detective. I hope being a human rights activist proves more exciting.

But this is enjoyable time together—Geoff's and my first chance to celebrate the end of our separation. His kisses are as sweet as I remembered.

"What was it like growing up in England?" I shift my weight so I don't get too uncomfortable on my makeshift cushion, but I make sure our bodies touch.

"Did I tell you Da sent me to an all-boy's school? They still have those in the U.K. if you can believe it."

"Really? Weird."

"It didn't seem strange then—I mean, it was my reality, wasn't it? But now it seems quite odd. So *last century*, don't you think?"

I agree, but I shrug at the same time to show I don't mind.

"It was fun, though. I always had mates to run around with. I got away with more in my spare time than I probably would have dared do at home. But I also studied hard, because it was expected of us. Turned out it was good preparation for grad school, so I really can't complain.

"At university, I was more of a loner. I learned not to mention my previous schooling or I'd get teased for being a *preppy.*"

I nod, and smile.

"Did you miss your parents?"

"My mum died when I was 10, and it was afterward that Da sent me off to school. I was lonely lot at first, but I got used to seeing Da on holiday. I think he needed the time to rebalance his life."

"I'm sorry about your mum."

"It was a long time ago. But afterward, I wanted more of Da's time than he could give. I think that's why we did so much together when I was at home. We're very close now."

* * *

About 7:40, the first person in the area gets into a car and drives off. Then several more leave. We get strange looks, but nobody stops to ask why we're here. They must make up some story about us that seem harmless. They look away when we kiss, so we do that a lot to keep them at a distance.

At 7:50, Douglas leaves the gym and walks quickly toward his van.

"Put on your helmet," Geoff says.

We throw my clothes back into the pack, and climb on our bikes. At first, on neighborhood streets, Douglas gets almost too far ahead for us to pursue. But once he turns onto the main street, despite the faster speed limit, the red lights let us to catch up regularly. We keep our heads down and stay back where we won't be recognized.

Just before 8:00 am, Douglas turns into the parking lot of a heating and air conditioning business. We wait a half hour before we conclude that he probably works here. Geoff decides to return just before 4:00 to follow him when he leaves.

I figure he's offering to go because he needs this whole detective act to be real. That'll mean I'm not a lunatic, and that our relationship has a chance.

"Thanks for trusting me—believing I wasn't crazy. I know it was tough when you heard I was in the looney bin. I chose the evaluation, just to be sure I was okay. I kind of fell apart after our fight."

"When you appeared at my window, all I wanted was a major hit of green, until you showed me the note. I was pretty shaky."

We kiss again. "Right now, I'm insanely famished. And not just for you."

Geoff laughs. Then we ride over to the IHOP.

"So," Geoff says when we've ordered. "We made progress this week. We know where Flexman lives, where he works, and that he was the likely instigator of the cross burnings. We don't know if his friend, Baldy, has a part to play in all this."

We pause as steaming breakfasts arrive at our table. Mine is coconut pancakes with a side of tangy pineapple syrup—deadly good. After a bite or two, I continue our list of information.

"We also know when Flexman visits the gym, and the names and addresses of the two men he tried to frighten." I stuff more food in my ravenous mouth.

"Peter Landsbury seems to believe us, and is checking the connection between what we learned and the hate crimes. I bet Jessica St. Marie has come 'round to our ideas as well, or will do, once she gets over being pissed." Geoff pauses for a bite of pecan waffle, and melted butter drips down his chin. I want to lick it off.

"The question is, will he escalate on his hate crimes, and if so, when," I think this through as I speak. "If he follows his previous pattern, it won't be until evening, and probably not until next weekend."

"Right. So let's take care of you next. What's your plan?" He tucks his last forkful into his mouth and sits back to chew.

"It's not 9:30 a.m. yet. I could make the hospital in time for all but one of my sessions. Right now, I'm an escaped mental patient. But turning up I'll be what—a penitent rebel?" I run the back of my fork through sweet goo and suck it off.

"Maybe an honest woman who made a personal decision to leave—especially if you catch the staff in a good mood. Tell you what. I'll ride over with you and make sure your bike gets home."

"What about James' bike? You'll leave it there?"

"Until I can get back to retrieve it. I could walk back to the hospital, or catch the bus, and have every minor concern. James won't care if it's gone for a few more hours. Might not even notice."

"I could tell the hospital staff that a dream made me do it." I snicker, and he laughs. It feels good to let my concentration go, to know someone else cares enough to keep an eye on me. We laugh together until nearby diners shoot us expressions of distaste.

Geoff leaves money on the table and we return to our bikes. "What if, when I follow Douglas today, I discover he's about to commit another crime?"

"Call the police first, then let me know. I'll find a way to join you." I sound confident though a dozen obstacles jump into my mind. "I hope my schedule remains unchanged. They might try to keep me another day. But I'm not sure they can without consent. Business hours are when the specialists work. So they should have most of the information that they planned to gather on me, already."

"Well, we can't get there any sooner than if we leave now." So we bike back to the hospital, slowing block by block, until we coast to a stop by its imposing entrance.

"Want me to go in with you?"

"That's crazy. I've gone to a lot of trouble to keep anyone from knowing that we got together while I was AWOL. I can check myself back in."

We have difficulty pulling back from our kiss.

"See you soon, Tiegen."

I nod, shoulder my backpack, and tromp up the stairs to the front door.

But once Geoff pedals out of sight, I have a heck of a job grabbing that door handle and pulling. And suddenly, my stomach is a mad hornet's nest.

I suspect this won't be fun.

Chapter 18

I return home at lunchtime, the same day. Hard to believe. The hospital staff were not pleased that I had left, but they supported my return to the program, making that the main message of the day. I told them I needed to get a message to a friend last night, and got no help from the nurse, so I left to make that happen.

My missed meeting was rescheduled for tomorrow. Seems like I'm far from the first mental patient to walk out. It's not like an asylum full of insane murderers — the type of place where security is intense. Only ordinary crazies end up there.

Like me.

* * *

When Mom picks me up, I consider not telling her. It seems the hospital can't give information to the parents of an adult patient without permission. But I decide to tell her anyway. I'm already hiding too much from her with all the amateur detective work. But I won't mention sleeping with the homeless.

Mom is livid. Although she keeps her lips pressed so tight they go pale from lack of blood, she manages not to explode until we are back at home in the living room.

"You sounded ready for this evaluation. Whatever made you leave before it was finished?"

"I had something I suddenly needed to do. I'm sorry, but I can't tell you what right now. But I will, once it's all figured out. I promise." I squint my eyes and focus my resolve.

"And why didn't you come home?"

"I did have time to argue with you. Sorry, but there is more of that story I can't tell you yet. It's all twisted into my decision."

"Dear, I'm afraid you are delusional, but don't realize it. You were pretty shut down when you checked in at the hospital. Now you sound grandiose. You seem seriously unwell."

"Mom, have I ever had delusions before, much less grandiose ones? Remember the adage 'the best predictor of a person's future behavior is their past behavior.' Instead of pinning some new label on me, because of the past twenty-four hours, why don't you give me the benefit of twenty-four years? Though it seems crazy to you, I know what I did and why. If I were in the same situation again, I'd make the same decision."

"Are you taking drugs? Or involved in something illegal? What made you act out, if you're not mentally diagnosable?"

"You know I hate drugs. And I've broken no laws. I'll explain when I can, Mom. I'm trying to help someone — two someones. But that's it. I can't say more."

"Right now, it's hard to trust you. Three days ago you agreed to a psych eval because you feared you were losing touch with reality. You couldn't get out of bed. I don't know what to believe and not believe. I really don't, Tiegen."

"I get that Mom. I do. I'm sorry I upset you. But the evaluation came out unchanged. I'm no crazier than I've ever been. Would it be better if I lied? I'm capable of that—saying something less weird than the truth to appease you. I wanted to tell the truth instead."

"In addition to upsetting us, you disappointed us. We thought we could depend on your judgment as an adult."

"You can. You'll see. I'm sorry Mom, but I had to do this. As an adult."

And so it went. I told the specialists at the hospital the same thing about not sharing everything yet. They took it better than Mom did. It's easier for them to think of me as grown up. But when I'm honest with myself, I have to wonder when I'll have that freedom to tell the real story to Mom or anyone else.

Yet the reports from the hospital were encouraging. I still appear sane in my own, odd, vivid-dream way. Dr. Crenshaw says I may have experienced a brief psychotic episode that was stress-related, but if so, it passed before my hospital stay. I only showed part of the signs.

Though still within the range, I'm past the most common age of schizophrenia onset, which is good news. I still screw up my life with bits of dream material. And the specialists can't help, other than to suggest a support group full of people with mental issues. If the group is full of Loony Luna's, I know it wouldn't help.

But then I wonder—what about the me in the mirror? My folks didn't try to take away the car or ground me, but when Mom looks at me now, I know she sees the child-me again, not the adult. I've lost ground, just when I thought we were beginning to treat each other like equals.

Transitions suck.

* * *

Monday, just before her shift ends, I give Jessica St. Marie a call.

"Did you see the list Douglas wrote, that I found at the library?"

"Yes. His names match the first names of the victims of the cross burnings. That helps, although they are common names in the Muslim community.

"But I heard that you and Geoff are doing your own detective work. Is that true?"

"You wouldn't follow up. So yes, to get the police onto the scene, we did. And I have more info. I can tell you Douglas' workplace now."

"You followed him? I have his address, his workplace, his priors and lots of other information now. Ask *me* if you have a question. Don't take any further risk, Tiegen. There's no purpose. None — do you hear me?"

"I hear you, but I'm not reassured. Will you stake him out so you can stop whatever he does next? It's going to get worse. That's my only purpose in staying involved. I'd sure rather hand our investigation over to you and go back to being an ordinary doctoral student."

The policewoman pauses, and I imagine machinery running in her head.

"We can't prove Douglas was the one who burned the crosses in those men's yards, but we're examining our evidence. Mrs. Nguyen, our criminalist has the crime scene data. She's excellent, so I expect results soon. The crimes appear related, because the wood, where it had been pounded into the ground, didn't burn completely. It is the same type at both houses. But that doesn't tie the crimes to our suspect."

"So you aren't watching him?"

"Not yet, no. At least, not every minute. We've scheduled regular drive-throughs in both his and the victims' neighborhoods Especially in the evenings.

"But both burnings occurred over the weekend. The suspect works 40 hours per week, so we don't expect he'll make any move until next weekend, at the earliest." The officer seems to choose her words carefully, and I wonder if she is limiting the information she gives me. Does she still mistrust me?

"Okay, good to know. Thanks for taking this seriously." I don't know what to do. I hang up and call Geoff.

"The police are still dragging their feet. But Jessica seems convinced Douglas won't move until the weekend. What should we do?"

"We've already gone way beyond what's reasonable, according to Peter Landsbury and her. Maybe we should let it go, at least until the weekend. Give the coppers a chance to do their work."

"If Jessica has nothing new by Friday, we could follow him after work—see if he does anything suspicious."

"Let's discuss it later. Are you going to the library tonight?"

"Nix on the library. That'll just draw me back into the case. I'll study at home this afternoon. Then may I come to your place after dinner?"

"Please do." He makes a kissing noise over the phone. "Ta."

* * *

"Do you miss tailing Douglas?" Geoff traces the line of my cheek down to my lips with his finger, and I shiver. I take hold of the finger and kiss it. We are sitting on the couch in James' living room.

"Umm. This is much superior. You know, I very nearly came back to your place last night. I dreamed that I had."

"And?"

"And we fell asleep in your bed spooned together. It was heavenly. I didn't want to believe it was a dream, when I woke up on the pine needles."

"You what?" His body statues still beside me.

Crap. I've put myself in a terrible position. Now he'll know I lied to him, unless I can cover this up. Pine needle print sheets, maybe? My mind scrambles.

"Tiegen, did you sleep outside last night?" His voice is so soft that I only hear it because his words are over-enunciated.

I hesitate just one moment before realizing that I must tell the truth. Even if it opens Pandora's box. I take a deep breath.

"Okay. Truth only from here on out. Yes, I slept behind the Recreation Center. Amanda was a lie. But what I said about sleeping here was true. I thought we'd get caught. So I made up a story to get you to go home."

"That is the stupidest thing I've ever heard, Tiegen. I can't believe you'd..." He splutters, sitting up beside me, his voice growing louder. "Do you realize the danger?" He breathes hard, his voice harsh. His eyes flash fire.

"I didn't realize it then. I mean, I figured if homeless people sleep outside, it can't be too awful. But when I woke up, a homeless guy was guarding me, afraid I might get trafficked into the sex trade. I didn't know trafficking went on in Woodsdale."

"It goes on in every city in the nation, or nearly. Can you really be that naïve—with your major?" His voice gets louder still.

"We studied the sex trade in class, with examples from Seattle—I just never thought about it in Woodsdale. So naïve?" I sigh. "I guess I was.

"You know, I quit watching TV and movies for years, because they colored my dreams. I read, instead. That way, I could look at the book in the morning and see precisely where my dream veered off the page."

"That's hardly an excuse. You endangered yourself..." He trails off, mid-sentence, and his breath quickens. He takes hold of my shoulders and turns me to face him.

"Tiegen, I want to ask a question, and I need your honest answer, okay?"

"What?" I straighten my backbone.

He takes my face in his hands and searches my soul. In his eyes, I see sad fear. My stomach clutches. *He's going to leave me for sure.*

"Tiegen, are you crazy?"

This is it. And I won't break my word and lie to him.

Chapter 19

"Honestly, Geoff, I-I don't know if I'm crazy or not. I don't think anyone knows. My doctor says I'm not, but always with a 'however' attached. If craziness is a continuum, I suspect I don't fall at either end." I look into his questing eyes and hope.

"That's the only answer I can accept." He trembles as he says this, then his eyes fill with tears. A single deep sob comes from his chest, and then he holds me, gripping like he never wants to release me. I squeeze him in the same way. We sit, clutched together, rocking back and forth for the longest time.

Gradually, we regain a sense of calm.

"I promise never to lie to you again," I say. "And I won't sleep like the homeless, either—that really was stupid, I admit. Stupid, but not crazy. They're not the same." I make sure he gets that before I go on. He nods.

"A lot of people who were important to me have let me down once they discovered that I was disabled. You and I were just getting over a fight that nearly ended our relationship. I didn't want to strain it again so soon and chase you away. You mean too much to me.

"I know excuses make no difference. I lied. Period. But that's what was going on." I look at the covers rather than into his face. I don't want to see that he's rejected me. The silence goes on and on.

"I understand, Tiegen. I'm holding you to your honesty, though. There's enough confusion with your dreams and reality getting muddled. I can't handle lies mixed in as well."

I look up at his face, and see he's still giving us a chance together. "I promise, Geoff. I don't break my promises."

He kisses me, and I kiss back, and soon we end up lying back on the bed, pressed together. His body is warm, firm, but giving in all the right places. I slip my hand up his back, under his shirt. Our kisses and touches are gentle, exploring. Time passes before we talk again.

"I've figured out some things about Jessica St. Marie," I finally say. "When she refused to take further action on the information I gave her, my opinion of her fell. I was disgusted that a policewoman would sit on her hands while a serious crime occurred nearby. I'd identified with her, and her inaction seemed wrong because it wasn't what I'd chosen for myself.

"But thinking it through, I realize that she has drawn a line for herself that she won't cross. She moves too darn slowly for my taste, but it's because she doesn't believe that ends justify means in an investigation. As a cop, she really values the law that says a person is innocent until proven guilty.

"Maybe I'm overinvested in this case because it has to do with human rights—an important concept of my major. But shouldn't I have a line I won't cross as well?"

"Definitely. I caught myself thinking about going onto his property to look for clues. I wanted to impress you as much as I wanted to catch Douglas. Then I caught myself — realized how much I need a break from the case. We are both over-involved."

"I know. But still, I worry that this weekend he may hurt Ibrahim or Mohammed. Keeping tabs on him then is still important to me unless the police take over his surveillance. After coming this far, I can't just give up."

"Then I'm with you, Tiegen."

* * *

Geoff and I keep our promise to stay away from Douglas before Friday. Each morning I check online for hate crimes from the night before, but nothing happens. Maybe the police understand criminals better than I think.

On Friday, fingers crossed, we check whether the police are staking out the HVAC facility where Douglas works. It appears they're not, so we follow him. He stops at a home and garden store for only five minutes. He must have known exactly what he wanted. We can't see everything he bought, because part of it is in a lumpy sack, but he clearly carries a fat bag of fertilizer.

We follow him home, but he doesn't go inside. Instead, the lights remain on in his garage for about an hour before he turns them out.

Probably it's his dinner time. Ours, too. Geoff's takes off for fast food nearby so we can keep up the surveillance.

When Geoff pedals back up the street with our food in a brown paper bag with green lettering, he passes in front of Douglas' house. As if he were spying on Geoff, Douglas' garage door rises and he calls out, "Hey you! You on the bike. Come over here."

My gut pinches at his words, but I see no way I can help except to stay hidden and keep my eyes open. I stare into the garage, which is crowded with boxes. A workbench holding power tools runs along the near wall, but I can't see all the way to the back wall. There are garden tools and a bucket, but nothing that makes my hackles rise. I wish I had brought binoculars.

Geoff looks back over his shoulder to see Douglas gesture to him, and gives him a wave. He keeps pedaling.

Then Douglas calls out, "Yes, you. Come here." Geoff's face flashes panic, but he gets off his bike, turns around, and walks it back toward the house at a brisk pace.

"Yes sir? What's up?" He keeps his voice cheery. His helmet is on, but his accent gives him away immediately. A sudden spear pierces me, and I shiver, though the evening is warm.

"Aren't you the guy from my gym?" Douglas asks.

"Which gym is that, sir?" Geoff asks, as Douglas' eyes rake him, up and down. Before Douglas can speak, though, Geoff feigns surprise, leans the bike against a tree, and in a few brief steps forward, extends his hand. "Of course, the health club. Sorry I didn't recognize you sooner. Small world, eh? Yeah, I'm pleased with the facility. State-of-the-art equipment. Good place for a workout, don't you think?"

Douglas, perhaps by reflex, shakes Geoff's hand, but doesn't speak. He squints his eyes, never looking away.

"Nice neighborhood. Convenient distance from the club." I imagine I know exactly which face Geoff shows to the enemy.

My gut clenches, the familiar pain kicking in. I can think of no way this can turn out well. I chew my lip. I hate waiting, unable to do a thing.

"Yeah," the man says. He sounds suspicious to me, but I'm hardly an unbiased observer. My stomach makes that clear. "Why are you here?"

Geoff lifts the hand containing the bag. "I felt a bit peckish. Supper time, you know. So I got some take out."

"And why come past my house with your food? Do you live nearby? On this street?"

"Not too near, but I like to ride the back streets home. Less traffic. More scenic, too." Geoff nods his head like he's agreeing with himself. I don't see Douglas nod. He continues to scowl at Geoff.

"Get off my street right now. Don't come back."

"Pardon me, sir? I think I misheard you."

"I don't want you near my house. In fact, I want you out of my neighborhood." Douglas amps up his volume to a roar.

"Now!"

Chapter 20

"Uh. Right. Whatever you say, sir. Cheerio then." Geoff backs up, turns his bike, and rides up the street past me, the bag of food in one hand. He doesn't turn his head as he passes. He doesn't hurry either.

I don't move until Douglas disappears back into his garage, and the door closes. Then I ride up the far sidewalk for the first block, before I get back on the street and put on some speed. I find Geoff at a corner about five blocks down. He gestures to me to turn his direction, left. I stop beside him.

"I'm glad you're all right," I jabber. "How did you stay so cool? I thought he was going to hit you — or something worse. That was scary."

Geoff takes the hug I offer. "Well, I smoked some green this afternoon before we got together. I'm sure it helped keep me mellow." He gives a little smirk before continuing.

"I find it interesting that the day Flex changes his habits, he's highly protective of his property. Makes me wonder what's hiding in his garage."

"Let's call the police again. Surely we have enough evidence now. This is their job, to stop him from committing another crime." My heart still pounds.

"There's a good chance that he'll strike again tonight." Geoff sets his mouth in a way I haven't seen before. He draws down his brow toward his nose while I jabber on.

"Does he know we tailed him? Maybe someone saw us studying his house and called him. He may have waited purposely to confront you. The garage door went up just as you passed his house."

"Call the police, Tiegen. If they come, lovely. If not, you know where to find me."

"You can't do this alone. If one of us gets caught, the other can go for help."

Geoff studies my face, and then his expression softens. "I don't want any awful thing to happen to you. But, yeah, we probably are safer together."

"Is there a different spot we can watch from? Somewhere less obvious."

"We could approach his house from the opposite end of this street—stay at the furthest distance where we can still watch."

I nod.

By the time we circle the block across the street from Flex, and find a new stakeout position, I'm far less worried about being noticed. I wish Jessica was in, but I'll take whomever I can reach. I dial.

"Peter? This is Tiegen Richards. Douglas's up to something in his garage. He bought a large bag of fertilizer, and he's been in there since he got home—about quarter to six.

His next attack may be tonight. He could really hurt someone. Please send an officer over here."

"Stay away from him, and quit playing detective! Don't force me to arrest you for stalking or trespassing or something you don't even know is a crime. You have no training for this. Leave that neighborhood immediately. Do you hear me?"

I hear him, but he didn't answer my question.

"If we leave, will you promise to watch his house? Absolutely? Because that's what it will take to send us home."

"'We?' Geoff's there, too? Staying hidden is harder for two. Are you in your car?"

"Um, no, on our bikes. But we're several houses down the street from Douglas. He shouldn't see us. We've been extremely careful." I don't mention Douglas' interaction with Geoff.

"I'm calling Officer St. Marie. One of us will get back to you soon. Meanwhile, put your phones on vibrate. You don't want to signal the whole neighborhood that you're on stakeout, okay?"

"Okay. As soon as we hang up." I gulp as I silence my phone. I hadn't considered my ring tone. I tell Geoff, and when he takes out his phone, I know he didn't think of it either. I wonder what other precautions we failed to take. My stomach pains worsen. Suddenly, I want to go home. I cross my fingers that we'll be relieved quickly. I'm ready to do something ordinary. Like watch police shows instead of criminals.

Ten minutes later, my phone vibrates. Jessica's tone is strained. I repeat the discussion, receiving her warnings to break off the stakeout and go home. I refuse again. It's easier the second time.

Then there's a long silence on the line that tells me she's thinking. I wait. "Let me get this right. You and Geoff will watch this suspect no matter what Officer Landsbury or I say, correct?"

"Yes. Until one of you takes over."

"You want a police officer to watch a man's house in case he's a terrorist?"

"Yes."

"I expect I'll regret this, but I'm on the way. Stay safe. I expect you to be so well hidden that you'll see me before I find you. I'm in civvies, and drive a blue Subaru. Watch for me in 10 minutes. Give me the closest house number to your hiding place."

I give her the number and describe the houses nearby as well as the tree we crouch behind. When I tell Geoff she's on the way, his smile spills relief across his face. He's frightened like I am.

"Brill, Tiegen, that's genius." He gives me a quick squeeze. Then, reassured, we hunker back down and wait for Jessica.

We talk in quick hushed voices, smiling nervously in expectation. I feel lighter, and Geoff's eyes dance now that we've finally won. His confrontation with Douglas frightened me more than I realized, because now I feel energy rise in me again.

Our new hide-out is superior to the first one. On this parking strip, between us and the curb, in addition to a tree to crouch behind we have a bush at our backs. Small trees in the yard beside us partially block us from the closest windows.

Of course, our bicycles are visible on the sidewalk side of the parking strip leaning against the tree, but if we're not seen, those could belong to anyone. As long as Douglas doesn't see them, I know we're safer hiding here.

I count the minutes since my talk with Jessica. She should arrive in five more minutes, I'd guess. She'll give us another lecture, but as long as we can convince her to stay, we'll have police involvement. That's more than we've had yet.

Geoff grins at me, and I grin back. Maybe we're not such horrible amateur detectives after all. The whole operation seems almost over now that help is coming. And we have a lot to explore together. A relationship to get on with. Desire rises in me at the thought of his body against mine.

Then, out of nowhere, a boot kicks me in the side, up under my rib cage, and I yelp. I roll onto my side and curl up, trying to breathe. I blink away the blotches before my eyes to see who the kicker is.

It's Douglas, of course.

Chapter 21

Douglas must've snuck out his back door, and then walked around the block in order to surprise us so abruptly. As I struggle to get my feet beneath me, he grabs the back of my t-shirt. He has Geoff in an arm lock and tries to control me with his other arm—keeping me off balance so that I can't rise.

I twist around and bite his arm until I taste blood. He curses, but he lets me go. The moment he releases my shirt, I put my two forearms flat to the elbow onto the ground behind me, pull up my knees, and aim a strategic kick towards his groin with my right foot.

Geoff curls out of the arm lock while Douglas focuses on me. Douglas has to grab Geoff with both hands and twist to have a chance of taking him down. They struggle so hard that my kick misses entirely as Douglas pivots Geoff to the ground in a wrestling hold. I push back from the fight, stand, and leap onto my bicycle, ready to ram or run, depending.

"Help! Somebody help us!" I yell, but no opens their front door. I yell again, and Geoff manages a yell, too, in the midst of his scuffle. I bend down and snatch up a rock, but I can't throw for fear of hitting Geoff.

"Geoff!" I hope for a pause in the struggle so I can cast my stone.

A dark blue car rolls up beside me. I'm so glad that Jessica has made it to us that I want to cry. "Geoff!" I cry again as the driver's door opens, and a figure races around behind me. I turn my head, but she has already passed my position.

In moments, I'm jerked to my right side, and I let my bike fall to the ground. I catch a toe in the spokes, and fall over, but instead of following my bike down, a shove uses my loss of balance to move me toward the street. I stumble along. A second push forces me onto my stomach, hanging out the back seat of the car, facing the far door. An iron grip seizes my right hand, and I hear duct tape tearing. I use my left hand to pull my body through the car toward the far door where I barely pull the door release, leaving the door ajar. The person behind me paws inside the car for my left hand. Rather than have my hands taped together, I grab the far edge of the seat and jerk hard, yanking myself a few inches farther inside.

My attacker gives up on taping my hands, and grabs for my ankles instead. But with two hands free I pull twice as hard for the far door. I draw up my knees and kick back like a spring, then retract them into a tuck. I hear a grunt as I hit and energy surges through me.

Crap. Despite my quick movement, a loop of tape now binds my ankles. My head hits the armrest of the far door as a person slips in beside me. The impact swings the door open, and I'm able to somersault myself outside and tumble to the ground. Sitting on my butt, I slam the door behind me.

I yell for help again, though I have little hope. As I lever myself up onto my bound feet, using the door handle, I see Douglas coming toward the driver's side door. I hunch my head, get my feet on the ground, and hop behind the car. A door opens, and then I hear grunting. I glance up and see a large mass being pushed inside the front passenger door. It slams, and Douglas vanishes back around the front. Then I hear the driver's door open and close. Within minutes of driving up, the car speeds down the street, leaving me behind.

The back passenger door opens and a startled face glances back at me, before the door slams, hiding Baldy's startled face. The car doesn't slow.

I survey the ground where Geoff scuffled with Douglas. All I see there is a spot of blood in the crushed grass. It must have been Geoff that Douglas pushed into the front passenger seat of his car.

While I try to figure everything out, I wrench hard at the duct tape that binds my ankles. I was lucky. I discover only one circle of tape around my legs. The roll hangs undetached from my leg, and I rip it away with a frantic swipe. Time whizzes away.

Finally, I stand on two unbound feet. I pull my bike off the ground, jump on, and peddle vigorously after the car that is just now turning a corner two blocks down the road. Might as well burn this adrenaline.

I stand on the pedals to gain more power. If that car gets away, I may never see Geoff again. They could kill him and conceal his body.

A part of my mind argues that I'm more likely to be caught than to release Geoff, but I don't slow down. I am a woman on a quest. Nothing will stop=. I couldn't bear it if anything horrible happened to him.

Using core muscles and body weight, I push the peddles hard, hard, harder.

My lungs singe; the bike speeds up.

Chapter 22

What I learned following Douglas before, helps me keep the car in sight now. I pant as I pedal, but I don't lose sight of it. I don't dare.

I know where the major streets cross. We should hit one soon. From my experience, stoplights make a vehicle easier to keep in sight, while other traffic on the road screens me.

So far, I doubt the men have spotted me. They're too far ahead and have Geoff to deal with. But I take greater care. Eventually, I know they'll look back out the window.

I turn onto the larger street, and catch a glimpse of Baldy's car several blocks ahead. Instead of riding the edge of the road, where I'd be more easily seen, I give a hand signal and pull in front of a green car, riding in the midst of traffic. As long as I hold no one up, I should be fine here — and tricky to locate.

I just need to sneak through the same stoplights as Baldy's car. Already I can tell that I'll miss the first one. I speed up and pass a couple of cars, but I called it—stuck behind a red light. Dang it.

I pull back toward the curb, passing cars on the right as they stop. I stop one car before the corner and stare ahead, wishing for x-ray vision, but too many vehicles turn in from cross streets and block Douglas and pal from view.

I chew my lip as I wait for the light to change. I hope they haven't turned. If I draw near them again, I vow to stay closer, regardless of the danger. I grind my teeth at the wait, willing the light to change.

When it does, I stay to the right, once again passing cars. One honks and I duck my head, horrified at attracting attention. I balance my speed with my progress after that, and keep my fingers crossed on the handle bars. I'd cross my toes, too, if that would help.

At the yellow light, cars slow again. I roll to a stop, staring ahead, hoping, hoping—

And there they are, only five cars ahead. Immediately I wave to the car behind me to my left and point in front him. As he comes to a stop, he leaves a little space for me, and I slip in, waving thanks. With one foot on the ground, I bend forward like a racer, so my profile is low. Hopefully, by now, they believe they've lost any pursuit.

Then, lungs screaming, legs pedaling like pistons, muscles shrieking for mercy, I'm off again.

Passing forward and back, left and right, I keep the car in view until it turns onto a deserted street. I stop before turning the corner and wait, because no other cars travel on that street. Just as I sneak forward onto the far sidewalk, where parked cars offer cover, Baldy's car pulls into a personal-storage facility's driveway. The gate opens, the car rolls inside, and the gate latches shut.

I ditch my bike between two giant rhododendron bushes and approach the self-storage. My every cell screams, "Beware!" Darting from tree to tree, I locate a spot where I can peer through the fence from hiding. But the aisle of storage units in sight has no cars parked along its edge. I find a safe spot for my next lookout. Again, I spy only an empty aisle.

On the third try, I spot the car, and pull my head back until I can barely see. The two men drag Geoff's body out of the car's front seat. He struggles feebly. I suspect he's injured, and my heart joins my stomach—aching. His hands and feet are bound. Although he's too far away to be certain, I think I see a flash of silver on the bottom half of his face. Guess his abductors keep multiple rolls of duct tape with them. Geoff won't break free without help.

The men balance Geoff on his bound feet long enough to shove him over into the container and lock it behind him. From where I stand, their movements are silent. I count the doors leading to the unit twice so I'm certain which one is Geoff's prison.

I dash back to my bike and crouch beside it, heart racing while I wait for their car to leave. Minutes pass, my stomach doing its icky thing. I wish I'd stayed longer where I could see. I shuffle my feet.

When Baldy's car finally turns toward me, I dip my head and freeze. So near to Geoff, it would be a disaster to be caught. But a vehicle passes, and when I peek, it is Baldy's car turning the corner.

I scurry back to the entrance and seek a way to pass through the gate. There's no way to open it: no pushbutton, speaker, or combination keypad. I pull and push on the gate. It rattles, but it doesn't budge.

"Hello?" I yell into self-storage desolation.

I wait and yell again.

Only silence answers.

Chapter 23

I crane my neck back to view the fence top. Nasty steel spikes, three inches apart, lance upward about eight feet, waiting to disembowel the unstable climber. Crossbars anchor the spears at the bottom, middle, and a foot from the top. Two cruel strands of barbed wire curl one below the other almost at the top, ready to gouge the flesh of anyone wary enough to avoid the spikes.

Chances are I can wedge my fingers into gaps along the middle crossbar and walk my feet up to meet my hands. With a toe wedged onto that bar, I might climb hand above hand while shoving with my foot. But I'm not sure I can get over the barbed wire and the spikes. I shudder. I have to try.

Swallowing my stomach, I rub my hands together, before grabbing the bars. The climbing goes okay, though my limbs tremble as I support my body on so tiny a foothold. My feet push me higher.

Then comes the hard part. I kick one leg up, trying to get it over the spiky coils, but my jeans catch and tear. Sharpened wires slice my leg, and I gasp in pain. I pull back to retrieve my leg, ripping the pants material away from the wire with one hand. I grit my teeth. No way am I going to get over.

Trembling, I slide back down, still on the wrong side of the fence. Blood streams from the burning slashes, but I doubt I'll bleed to death before I can rescue Geoff. A patch of denim flutters above me from the barbed wire—the flag of the victor. I scowl at it, and get out my cell.

"Officer St. Marie? It's Tiegen. I'm at a self-storage where Geoff is being held prisoner. I'm trying to figure out how to get inside."

"I nearly lost it when you weren't where you said you'd be on stakeout. I sure don't like your involvement in this case.

"Which storage center is it?"

I give her the name and the streets bordering the closest corner, and she promises to find it.

I limp as fast as my sore leg can go, following the perimeter of the fence, hoping for a second entrance. I need to find a place where somebody will hear my yell. The facility is enormous; I see no break in the barbed wire. The fence protects square blocks of units, served by only one driveway. I turn the corner. Again, it has only one driveway with a gate, identical to the last one. Except for the three-inch gap between each edge of the gate and the continuation of the fence, the barbed wire is ubiquitous.

I turn the next corner, my leg less sore, and skip-jog down the sidewalk studying the fence. At the center of this side are side-by-side gates. I sprint over to examine them more closely. A "ring for service" sign and a button to the left of the two gates reward me. I push the button, and hear a buzz.

I wait about 30 seconds. I cross my legs, pushing my injured calf against the good one to stop the bleeding. My jeans are streaked red.

Then I reach out and push the buzzer again, twice. I almost despair, but a boomer, with a gray beard that matches his long ponytail, limps toward me.

"Help! I need your help!"

Without opening the gate, he peers through the bars at me. "The business office is across the street." His breath reeks of gum disease, and my nostrils try to clench shut. "What do you want?"

"My friend was kidnapped." I shriek, my patience expended. "He's locked up inside. Let me in there now!"

Squinting, the man takes a slow, careful look at my face, my bloody leg, my body and back to my face. "So, how did he get here? And why are you bleeding?" His intense face brings up a sick image of the psych intern with his groping desire, and I gulp back bile. But this guy is my best bet to reach Geoff, so I have to convince him. I tell him the truth.

"I ditched my bike on the far side of the block and followed the fence around to here. When I tried to climb over, I cut my leg. So now I'm begging you — please let me in. My friend is locked in a storage unit. He's tied up and hurting."

"You tried to break into this facility, and now you think I'll open the gate for you?" He huffs and shakes his head, taking his teensy fleck of power in this world seriously.

"I admitted it to you, because I had good reason. What reason will you give the authorities if Geoff smothers in the unit while you give me a hard time out here?" I glare into his eyes, pulling myself to my full height.

He ponders this for a moment. "Which unit?"

"I can figure it out from over by the other gate. I counted the doors. Please, please hurry. He needs your help right away."

"Put your hands over your head and turn around slowly. Are you carrying any weapons?"

"None." I turn. The skin on my neck shivers when I turn my back to him.

Then I hear the music of a gate swinging open. "Come on in and prove it." He pulls out a cell phone and places a call. "I'm admitting a woman." He turns to me. "Speak your name." He, holds out the phone.

"Tiegen Richards," I enunciate into the phone.

"Show me picture ID."

I'm nearly batty from the delay, but I hold myself in check and pull my driver's license from my pants pocket. The guard takes a long look at the license, looks up at my face again and nods.

"Now freeze," he orders. I do, and he snaps a picture.

Then he speaks into the phone again. "ID verified," he says. He clips his cellphone back onto his belt.

I step forward, but the guard stops me. "I have to pat you down, first." His tone is gruff. I try to force the grasping hands of the intern out of my mind. I press my lips together, stick my arms out to the sides, and only jump a little as I feel him touch my sides. When he reaches up between my thighs, though, I stifle a scream.

"Lead me to the unit in question. And tell me your story again while we walk."

Surprisingly unmolested, I talk. It distracts me. Though his limp is no worse than mine, the guard chooses the pace of a stroll. In my head, I coach myself to be patient. But I imagine cracking a whip at him. Mush!

We finally reach the right row, and I ask the guard to wait while I count doors. I count twice to make sure I've made no mistake. Then I knock on one and call out, "Geoff?" My reward is the sound of kicking against door from inside.

"He's in there," I tell the guard, who still moves slowly despite the noise.

The sound raises the guard's eyebrows, and he fumbles with his bulky set of keys. Not hopping up and down while I wait takes tons of self-control.

The guard opens the door. "What the hell?" He steps inside to where Geoff lies on his back. He has maneuvered into position on the cement floor where he can kick the door. His tape-bound feet are drawn back for another strike.

I push past the guard. I peel the tape off of Geoff's mouth before the guard kneels at Geoff's hands, takes out a pocket knife, and with a couple of strategic swipes of the knife, cuts the tape.

"Ouch! I've never been more glad my university frowned on facial hair," Geoff says when his mouth is free. "I shan't need a shave today." He rubs his face where the tape had been.

I laugh, and stroke his face once, then move down to his feet. The guard arrives at the same time and cuts the bonds. Geoff sits up and rends the remnants of tape off his legs. My heartbeat finally slows toward normal.

"How did this happen?" The guard's face is ashen. His voice shakes. I like him a lot better now that he has dropped his official demeanor. He looks worried—maybe even sorry he put me through the hullabaloo while Geoff lay bound and gagged.

While Geoff explains, I call Jessica and let her know I got in. She is on her way. As I finish, Geoff touches his injured forehead and examines his fingers.

"They bonked me hard, and I was too out of it to fight when they pushed me into the car." Sticky blood marks his temple, but it no longer flows.

"I tried to fight Douglas so you could get away. But once two of them were after us, I could only rescue myself."

"I saw you hop toward your bike just before the car zoomed off. Douglas was a block away before he realized they'd lost you. He blew up at Baldy, but by then Baldy was busy taping me up, so they just drove on. I don't know if either one got a good look at your face."

I realize we both still wear our helmets. "Here's hoping I'm lucky."

"Can you stand?" the guard asks Geoff.

"Of course." Geoff sounds as if he can't imagine being unable to stand. He struggles to rise, but he's weak. Both the guard and I hold out a hand. Geoff takes them both and pulls himself up. He winces, but stands, swaying a bit as he presses his hand against the cut on his head.

"Here, lean on me," the guard says. "I have an office where I watch the camera feed between rounds. I can give you a cup of coffee and a Tylenol there."

"Exactly the thing. I don't suppose you have cakes to go with that?" Geoff winces as he looks down at his blood-spattered clothes. "But plainly, I'm not dressed for tea."

Chapter 24

Even though our pace is slow, Geoff depends on the guard for balance at first. By the time we reach the tiny office, though, he walks on his own. I take his hand, and the feel of his pulse against mine makes me want to weep. I could have lost this man.

Not long after the guard rinses the coagulated blood off Geoff's cut head, and my sliced leg, he pours us each a cup of thick, bitter coffee from a dark-stained pot.

My cell rings. Jessica asks how to reach us from the street. I hand the phone to the guard, who directs her to the main gate, which he promises to open for her, and from there to his office.

The policewoman shows up quickly. The moment we catch her up on recent events, she calls Peter and asks for a stakeout on Douglas' house.

"Thanks for the Tylenol and the plaster," Geoff says.

"Plaster?" the guard asks.

"Oh — the bandage."

"Of course. The least I could do."

We climb into Jessica's car and leave the mini-storage quickly.

"Now I will take you both home." Jessica speaks in her no-nonsense voice.

I start to respond, but she cuts me off. "Not an arguing point, Tiegen." Her voice snaps.

"Well, I can't go home without my bike," Geoff says. "It's borrowed."

She mutters something like, "I should know better." Then she picks up my bike, pops off the front wheel in about two seconds, and shoves both parts into the back of her Subaru. It is a lighter blue than Baldy's car, and smaller. She takes off for Douglas' house with us in the back seat.

"Keep your heads down when we arrive. And no exiting the car for any purpose. Pee in there if you need to. Got that?

"If there's shooting, you'll be safest on the floor. I expect this will a quick stop, but if not, I want you both hidden. Any distraction will split my concentration and put us all at risk. I am serious about this. Agreed?"

Geoff's eyes lock with mine, and I see the reflection of my terror in them.

This time, we follow orders.

* * *

When St. Marie arrives back at Douglas' house, Peter has it staked-out—professionally this time. On his seat sits a vegetable and dip tray from the supermarket. I raise my eyebrows. As odd as it looks, it has to be better for him than doughnuts.

"Down. Now," Jessica says. We scooch down low.

She exits our car and walks over to Peter's unmarked cruiser. I crack the window to listen, but I keep my head low.

"No sign of him," Peter says. "Nobody else has come by either. But I'll continue the watch."

"Good work. Which is more important—to get a crime scene team on site where the abduction occurred, or to continue the stakeout in case he returns?"

"Stakeout. Right now, no one seems likely to contaminate the scene. And if the suspect sees cops on his return, he'll run before we can pick him up. There's a good chance he doesn't know that Geoff's been released."

"Agreed. Any idea where he's gone?"

Peter shakes his head. "No clue."

"I have an idea where he might be," I tell her when she climbs back into her car. "Woodsdale Islamic Center. He wrote it on that note I picked up."

"The Center is on the way back to your house, so I'll drive by for a quick look. They have a Friday evening gathering. Many local Muslims attend it."

She pulls out, but Geoff asks, "What about my bike?"

"If you can do without it a bit longer, I'd like the Criminologist to examine the area of the abduction before anything's moved."

He grunts, but doesn't comment. Knowing it's James' bike, I can imagine his concern.

* * *

At Woodsdale Islamic Center, the tiny parking lot is packed. Cars line the road wherever parking is permitted. Jessica pulls into a church parking lot, a couple of blocks up the hill, and demands that we remain in the car.

The church has something going on, too, because the parking spaces closest to the building are taken, along with a few in the row beside the road, where we park.

"I'll take a quick walk," Jessica says. "Stay put."

"Do you have the description of Douglas' van?" I ask.

"My radar is on high alert for it." She taps the side of her forehead twice.

We wait in the car, but I stare out the side window at her receding figure for as long as I can—concerned for her, wishing I were her. She vanishes along a tiny cement walkway toward the entrance. It's set back from the street—all but its sign.

I sigh and lean back to wait—a most common non-activity lately. Geoff smiles at me and takes my hand. When I look at him I see that the place where he was hit sports a big lump near his temple. It's my turn to wince.

"I hope that doesn't feel as bad as it looks." I reach across my body to lightly touch the knot.

"It's not so bad. Makes me feel like 'Bond. James Bond.' Just need the togs."

"We're far from spies. I didn't even realize I'd left my ringtone on during our stakeout until I was reminded." I shake my head. "How did we get so mixed up in this investigation?"

He bends over and gives me a tender little kiss. "Adventure bringing you down? It's lasting much longer than we planned, isn't it?"

"That's part of it. But when I saw you stuffed into Douglas' car, almost like a dead body, and then he drove away, things got real. I never pedaled as hard as I did trying to keep you in sight on the way to the self-storage. I couldn't let those men take you from me."

"I felt like that when I left you at your friend's house the other night. I kept wondering if I'd done right. But I wanted to trust your judgment. I dreamed that night that I'd lost you in a dark cavern. When I called out, and you answered, your voice grew farther and farther away until it vanished altogether." He ran his fingers through my hair. "That was a dark night for me."

"I guess that's what happened, sort of. But in my dream, you had an arm across me in the warm darkness. The sweet things you said felt like caresses."

He startles, and looks into my eyes.

"And that memory is as real to me as sleeping outside. It's my favorite memory of you, even if it never happened."

His lip quivers for a second as he gives me a vulnerable smile.

"It doesn't have to be just a memory."

I glow inside at his words.

We lose ourselves in kissing, and when I look up, the windows are fogged. I giggle as I point it out to Geoff.

"Aha, privacy!" His mouth twists into a comic leer.

A car pulls up beside ours. "The cops just heard you." I try to look serious.

"Bloody coppers." He growls the words, but he's laughing too.

"It's probably Peter." I wipe a little circle clear on my window and peer out.

I gasp.

Douglas steps out from the driver's side of the van parked beside us.

Chapter 25

"On the floor now!" I shove Geoff's shoulder down hard.

He arches his eyebrows. "I like your enthusiasm, but we've no need to rush."

"No!" I whisper. "Not that."

I dive for the floor with my back against the car door and make a wild gesture to him from there.

"Douglas just parked beside us. And I breached our privacy by clearing a peephole in the fog. Get as far out of sight as you can!"

He readjusts quickly, laying his head in my lap on the floor while forcing his legs to grasshopper into the tiny space. "How did he find us?" Geoff imitates my volume.

"I'm not sure he did. I think he's on his way to the Islamic Center and couldn't find closer parking, just like us. As long as he doesn't see the break in the window-fog, we may be okay. Just don't move." My whisper is so soft that I fear Geoff can't hear me. At least Douglas won't.

"Righto."

We stay frozen for five minutes, before my muscles cramp. "Do you think he's gone?"

"Wait a tad longer, just to be sure."

We both listen. I hold my breath. There. Is that footsteps? I put my finger against Geoff's lips. My heart thuds.

Suddenly, the front door opens, and I am afraid to let out my breath. I freeze, aching for air. Then we hear a voice.

"Tiegen? Geoff? Are you here?"

I release a small explosion, and refill my lungs, as Geoff scrambles up onto the back seat. He reaches a hand down to me.

"Brilliant timing, officer."

It is Jessica St. Marie.

"Why are you two on the floor? Did you hear gunfire?" Jessica's weapon is in her hand. She speaks to us, but her head swivels every direction as she checks the area for movement.

"That's Douglas' van." I gesture with my head. "I was afraid he'd see us."

"Nobody's here that I can see. Where did he go?"

"Um, the Islamic Center?" I wonder if I'm right. "I heard only one door slam. I don't think he's carrying much."

"Was he armed?"

"I don't know. I just saw him for a second, before I hid," Great detective I am.

"No worries. You did the right thing. I'll take a look around here. I'm locking the car. Stay inside and keep your heads low." She takes off.

"What if there's incriminating stuff in his van?" I look at Geoff.

"Then, he'll be back for it. We could sneak a look."

"Let Jessica do it. I'm staying right here." I still shiver from the shock of the car door opening, so I cuddle up against Geoff while we wait.

The locks click open, and Jessica slips in. "There's a meeting in the church, but nobody else is around. You may be right about where he went, Tiegen. Those are peaceful people. He better not be carrying."

"Did you look in his windows? With a torch?"

"I looked, but not with a light." She takes a flashlight from her glove compartment and flicks it on. She climbs out, leaving her door ajar, and walks around the suspect's van, shining her flashlight into the interior. Then she returns. "Nothing special. If anything's there, it's hidden well."

"So, still no hard evidence." I sigh. After all the waiting, I'd hoped for more.

"Well, he kidnapped Geoff and attempted to kidnap you. And the knot on Geoff's head is evidence of assault. If I find this guy, I have plenty to hold him."

She picks up her phone. "Peter? Any news?" She listens for a minute, and then summarizes what we've been through.

"I need back-up to apprehend him when he returns. And I'd love a warrant to search his van. For his garage and house, while you're at it." She listens. "Thanks, Peter. Get here as soon as possible." She hangs up.

"So what now?" Geoff squirms on the seat.

"We wait. I'm not leaving you alone. Backup's on the way."

Silent for a minute, she looks from me to Geoff and back. "I don't suppose you two want to tell me how you fogged up my windows so thoroughly?"

* * *

Jessica moves her vehicle up the row, half the parking lot away from Douglas'. When Peter arrives, she has him park beside Douglas' van, but leave two empty spaces between them.

The officers plan together in soft voices. Then Peter gets back into his car on the passenger's side. He pulls the door closed, but leaves it unlatched, and turns off the dome light. Jessica crouches outside the passenger side of our car. Geoff and I duck back out of sight.

As if on schedule, the quick pace of footsteps echoes in the night. Doors creak open, and I risk a peek out of the hole I rubbed in the fog. Douglas hauls out a canvas bag from the back of the van. It's stretched full of bulky shapes. The way he stands looks like he counterbalances a fair amount of weight.

He startles when Jessica says, "Set down the bag slowly, back up two steps, and put your hands on top of your head."

Douglas does. "Who are you?"

"An officer of the law and an excellent shot. As a matter of fact, Officer Landsbury, off to your left, is also an excellent shot. If you do exactly as I say, we won't have to prove it."

I hear voices approach across the parking lot. People must be streaming from the church building towards us; their meeting ended. I rub my peephole a little wider.

But the officers don't look away from Douglas. "I'm going to cuff your hands behind your back. I'm arresting you on suspicion of kidnapping and assault." Jessica says.

She glances at Peter, who nods. Then she holsters her firearm, grabs the suspect's right hand and clamps a handcuff onto his wrist. She reaches for his left hand in what should be a routine movement.

But just then, a bright pink ball rolls into a parking spot between the two officers. A girl of about six follows it, her long jet hair trailing behind. She doesn't see Peter until after she picks up the ball. Then she freezes right in front of him, looking at his gun with wild eyes. He can't fire.

Douglas twists out of Jessica's grasp and sprints toward the front door of his van, handcuffs dangling from his wrist.

She grabs her gun, but he's inside before she can get a bead on him.

He starts it up, and backs right towards Jessica, who jumps out of the way. Douglas turns the van and races out of the driveway. Then, with a screech of tires, he turns southeast down the street.

But Peter reacts swiftly—jumps into his car, backs out, and follows swiftly: siren blaring, lights flashing. They both take off down the street at high speed, until they vanish out of sight.

I feel a touch on my shoulder and turn to see Geoff, attempting to see over my shoulder and through my small peephole. He looks worried and squeezes my shoulder. I wipe madly at the window with my palms, and pull Geoff over where he can watch as well.

Jessica makes a quick call on her cell, then gets yellow emergency tape out of the trunk, and ropes off the area where Douglas' vehicle sat a moment before. Stepping inside the tape circle, she uses the muzzle of her gun to lift open the mouth of the canvas bag. She glimpses something inside, and her face goes pale. She gently rests the fabric back where it had been.

"I've got to know what's in that sack." Geoff pushes open the car door and eases out of the back seat, leaving the door open behind him.

"What is it?"

Her answer makes him stiffen. I feel chills down my spine.

"Explosives."

Chapter 26

It is going to be another late night.

Two bomb squad specialists come to examine the explosives and make certain they won't detonate if taken back as evidence.

Mrs. Nguyen, the criminalist from the PD, arrives and collects crime scene data. In addition to taking the explosives, she looks for footprints, and vacuums up everything in the part of the lot where we all parked.

Mrs. Nguyen appears forty-something and wears wild clothing and stacked heels. Jessica opens her trunk so Nguyen can go over my bike for trace evidence from the fight before the kidnapping. Nguyen is so meticulous, even vacuuming out the trunk, that I wonder if I'll ever get my wheels back.

Worse, she's visiting the kidnap scene next, and plans to go over Geoff's bike before he rides it again. Geoff and I raise our eyebrows at each other. No way James' or my parents will believe we were safe from danger if we come home without our bikes—because they're being held as evidence by the P.D. We'll just have to stick this out until Nguyen finishes.

She also takes samples of our hair, vacuums fibers off our clothes, and has us swab the inside of our cheeks for genetic comparison to any body fluids she may come across. Even knowing that she gathers evidence to arrest Douglas and Baldy, and that I have nothing to hide, I squirm at her thoroughness.

The detective, Anders Johanson, is a good-natured Scandinavian-American around thirty, whose coloring is about as light as it can get without being albino. He talks individually with Geoff, Jessica and me.

Joy, joy. We get to repeat everything we told Jessica as well as describe all that just happened in the parking lot. Guess Jessica will find out what we were doing to steam up her windows. It's not like we did anything wrong, but I don't usually talk about personal stuff with people I hardly know. I enjoy my privacy. My stomach pinches.

In the middle of all the activity, a reporter and photographer from the Herald show up. They heard about the party on the police scanner. They want pictures of Geoff and me next to the Islamic Center's sign for tomorrow's newspaper. So, tired as we are, we pose.

Meanwhile, Jessica and Peter keep in close touch via police radio. We listen, too. Through the Woodsdale city streets, Peter has little trouble keeping Douglas in sight. Then he calls for back-up.

"This is Benjamin Mulback moving into place two blocks to the northwest," one officer says on the radio. Another bookends the chase to the southwest. I hear their sirens over the air until they establish a presence on the nearby roads.

"Landsbury here. Just missed a light that the suspect squeaked through. Suspect still headed east."

"Roger. Turning into your street two blocks ahead. Suspect's van in view. Will turn off when you are back in place," Benjamin Mulback says on the air.

After a few minutes of silence Peter says, "Following again."

"Roger that. Turning off." The three vehicle pursuit plaits together with such skill, following the route that Douglas takes, that the suspect is unable to break away. I want to cheer.

"Suspect just took on-ramp to Interstate 5 off 196th. I'm right behind," says Peter. "No longer attempting to stay out of sight. I have a full tank. Hope he doesn't." Then the transmissions stop. I imagine the chase continuing along the Interstate. My mind fills with speeding cars and screeching tires.

Jessica puts my bicycle back in her trunk, and we head to Douglas' house again, where Geoff picks up his bicycle from Nguyen. She has completed whatever magic she does. As we leave the police car we hear one last interchange on the radio.

"Suspect just made a quick turn off the interstate, but I'm right behind him," Peter speaks in quick tempo. His voice sounds higher when he says, "He squeeked through the light off the exit ramp, but I'm trapped. I turned on my siren and lights, but traffic is too dense for me to reach the intersection.

"Crap. I've lost the suspect," Peter reports a moment later. "I hope I can pick him back up at the next light." A thudding sound comes through the radio along with his voice, and I imagine him pounding his steering-wheel.

That is the last Geoff and I hear. As much as we want to know the conclusion of the chase, we are yawning tired.

So finally, we peddle home, after midnight, to our respective houses. I can hardly stay awake. Geoff has to be aching as well.

* * *

I sleep in, the following morning, but still awaken groggy. Before I get out of bed, I call Jessica to hear what happened after we left her. She suggests that Geoff and I come to the office for a debrief and promises to share the latest news.

We arrive together, in my car. The receptionist watches for us and escorts us to a large interview room. Jessica and Peter soon join us, along with Criminalist Nguyen, Detective Johanson, and Benjamin Mulback who assisted in the pursuit of Douglas last night.

"Thanks for coming in, Geoff, Tiegen," Jessica says. "We all know chunks of this story, but nobody knows it all. I thought it would be easiest if we ran through it from beginning so we all have the same information. Since Tiegen first recognized that a crime was being planned, I'd like her to review the early facts." She turns to me. "Go ahead."

I repeat my part of the story, and am the major speaker for ages while Geoff, Jessica and Peter throw in bits of information. It seems Peter was the officer who doubted my story initially. He asked Jessica to check with Geoff.

I tell them about surveilling the men at the library, the gym and at Douglas' house.

"What made you kids think you had the ability for such dangerous work?" Benjamin asks.

"We are not kids. And we never assumed we had the skills. We did it because it sounded like the police wouldn't follow up without more evidence." I thrust my chin forward. "I couldn't let two people get hurt."

Quiet encompasses the room for a long moment.

Then Detective Johanson takes over the meeting.

"Obviously, we had a disconnect here. As police, we require evidence to proceed. Hearing that, Geoff and Tiegen took action based on what they had witnessed. They worked without experience or training, but with a conviction that innocent people were at risk. In their naivety, they acted rashly. Yet they did surprisingly well. Lack of our support actually led to their risky behaviors.

"Once this case closes, we will reconvene to discuss how better to handle similar cases in the future. Right now, let's get back to the events of the case." He nods to Jessica, who takes up the story.

"When I finally agreed to join Tiegen and Geoff, it was almost too late. I reached the suspect's house and found that Geoff had been kidnapped. Tiegen had followed the car on her bike in hopes of rescuing him. Because of her bravery, I was able to join them once she gained access to the storage facility."

Peter Landsbury reported losing the suspect after a chase to Marysville. "I issued an all-points bulletin on the make, model and license number of the van. We searched Marysville, joined by their police and several county sheriffs, but did not locate the suspect's vehicle. We did, however, mount a watch on the suspect's house."

"I assume he didn't go to Baldy's house?" I ask.

A silence falls while one person looks to another around the room.

"We don't know his real name or address," Jessica says. "Do you?"

Geoff shakes his head. "But you can get it from the owner of the gym, right?"

"I know where he lives." My voice shakes. "I followed him home once."

Geoff catches his breath. His look of betrayal makes me turn away.

"I don't know the address, but I can lead you there," I say.

The next thing I know I'm in Jessica's police cruiser, directing her to Baldy's house. When I tell her we're in the neighborhood, other police block off the escape routes.

Then something strange happens. The streets we turn onto are suddenly unfamiliar, and the house I am looking for doesn't match the age of the surrounding structures.

Jessica drives a grid pattern through the area, and when I recognize a street, we follow it. Shortly afterward, I no longer know where I am.

She continues the grid where she left off. But over and over again, we make a turn and I lose my way. I can't recognize anything from my previous trip to Baldy's.

"I hate to say this, but I don't think I've ever been here after all." I feel blood color my cheeks.

Her head turns sharply to me, but her face is open. "You said that you knew the way. Did you dream that, too?"

I can't speak, but I nod my head yes. My eyes flood, and I try not to blink so the tears stay captive.

She stops the car. "This is the part you couldn't tell me, right?"

I swallow. "Right. I have a disability. My dreams are as real to me as waking life. Sometimes I mix them up." My voice sounds low and shaky.

"Do you foretell the future from your dreams?"

"You mean, like a medium or something? You're kidding. The way my life goes, I don't see the present clearly, much less the future. My dreams are no gift, believe me."

"And you didn't tell me because--?"

"Because you already doubted me. If you knew about my dreams, I figured you'd dismiss my report outright." Misery overcomes me, and tears slide down my cheeks.

"You may be right." Jessica's voice is now soft as well. "But I would have been wrong." She picks up her radio.

"Let's call off the search. Tiegen is unsure of the location. We may be in the wrong neighborhood. Let's try something else, like old fashioned police work, to find the suspect's friend. St. Marie out."

"Don't worry," she says. "I have no need to share your secret with the others. It won't change the way we approach this case."

"I appreciate that," I whisper.

* * *

Geoff comforts me when we get home. At least I only had to tell one person, Jessica, about my dream disability. Only one more person who'll think I'm psycho.

"Geoff, you better work with the police during the rest of the case. You don't make mistakes like I do."

"Come here, sweet dreamer." He bundles me into a hug. "Look at how much we've accomplished. Those explosives could have killed many people at the Islamic Center. And if Douglas goes home now, he's nabbed. His van is on file with every police and sheriff's office in the state, and it's pretty certain the police will track him down. We did what we set out to do. More than that, don't you think?"

I have to admit that he's right. "But it would have been better if I had kept my dreams corralled. I felt so stupid when the police followed Jessica and me to what was supposed to be Baldy's house. I was so sure I knew how to get there, but I failed. My dream created the final streets and the actual house. I felt terrible each time familiar streets turned strange and I was lost."

"Shh. Without your dedication from the beginning, the police wouldn't be involved at all. You know that. You are my hero."

I put my arms around him and hug back. Having someone who believes in me makes failure bearable.

"Hey. Come over to my house. James and his family won't be back until late. They're in the mountains for the day. I was going with them until the police called to ask if I'd be around.

"It would be just we two there. We could recreate your special dream together. It sounded like a lovely thing."

I nod, glad to get away from the intrigue.

And ready to make a good dream come true.

* * *

In the middle of the night, back in my own bed, an unusual sound awakens me. Someone taps at my window. I jump up, expecting Geoff. I open the blinds and then crack open the window. I can't see clearly, so I put my face up to the glass. With screen behind it, I don't see much at first. My nose touches as I stare out, leaving a tiny patch of fog.

Then I jerk back as fast as I can and slap a hand over my mouth, half-stifling a shriek.

Douglas' face stares at me, monstrous and distorted where he's pushed it up against the other side of the screen.

Chapter 27

I slam closed the window and pull the blinds before realizing I would be better off if I could see what he's up to. But when I reopen the blinds, he has vanished.

With shaky fingers, I speed-dial Geoff.

"Douglas is outside my house. He just looked in my window." My voice shakes.

"Shite! He must have recognized you at some point, after all. I'm coming. Wait." I hear him clatter around. Then he says, "I'll call you back as soon as I'm on my bike, okay?"

"Okay. Hurry, please."

"Absolutely. Is your phone on vibrate?"

"Yeah. Remembered this time. Yours too, just in case."

"Got it."

Geoff hangs up and I dial 911. The operator promises to send a police car, fast. I warn him that the police shouldn't shoot anyone, because my boyfriend may be outside, playing at being Daniel Craig.

Geoff's back on the phone in about five minutes, but it seems like hours. I've never been so glad to hear his voice.

"So Tiegen, Is Douglas armed?"

"I don't know. All I saw was his face. I nearly woke everybody up by screaming, but just stopped myself."

"How did he find you, anyhow?" I hear his breath quicken, and I know he is peddling hard now.

"He must have gotten my name from the article in the Herald today, then looked me up in the phone book. I'm listed. My folks still have a land line."

"Right. So, I'm approaching your house. I'll stash the bike and keep out of sight."

"Don't go after him yourself. This time, the police are on the way."

"I'm just going to sneak over by your window. I want to be by your side until this is over. I don't want him getting into your bedroom."

I want to tell him not to come closer, that I can run to my parents if Douglas breaks in, but part of me is relieved that he's nearby. I don't manage to speak before he appears outside my window. I open it and whisper to him through the screen, our lips only inches apart.

"You shouldn't have taken the risk, but I'm so glad you're here. The police should show up any time. Be cautious, okay?"

"Of course." He puts his hand onto the screen and I put mine against it. I can feel the cold of his palm against my warmer one.

A siren sounds in the distance. I exhale, feeling safer. "Hear that?"

"Yes. It's almost over, Tiegen. You're safe. He'll run when he hears them."

He pauses, then adds, "Your hand is warm." He puts his other hand onto the screen. Again, I place mine against it. We gaze at each other, almost touching.

The siren shrills, and lights flash, growing larger as they approach. "They're here," I let out a breath of air I must have held deep inside.

"See? I told you that you'd be..."

Behind Geoff, so swift that I can't warn him to run, a knife flashes up and then down into his back.

Wet thuds fill my ears.

"No!" I scream, but the knife rises and falls again. Geoff collapses to his knees, and before his head falls forward, I see disbelief frozen on his face. Behind him Douglas crouches, bloody knife dripping in his hand, and then looks to the side at the police car. He slashes my window screen with an animalistic growl.

I slam the window.

"Put your hands up and don't move," a voice calls out from the street. But Douglas, in one step, disappears toward the back of the house.

"Over here!" I yell as I open the window and push out the ruined screen. "Here! Someone's hurt!" I yell again as I cast aside the aluminum frame and put a foot up on the window sill so I can climb outside.

A hand appears, and helps me down outside. "Is this the victim?" the policeman asks.

"Yes." I kneel by Geoff's head, leaving room for the officer to reach him. "He was stabbed twice. No more than a minute ago. I don't know how anyone can survive an attack like that."

"Is the assailant nearby?"

"I think so," I say, and he picks up his radio.

"Assault victim down. Assailant still in area, armed with a knife. Call for an ambulance and back-up. Then initiate search."

Geoff is still half on his knees, but his head and shoulders have fallen over to the side. The ground pulls his mouth all twisty. He appears unconscious. With light coming through the window I see blood everywhere—more all the time.

"Go back inside. I'll care for the victim," the officer says.

"His name is Geoff. I can help stop the bleeding."

The officer pulls Geoff flat onto his stomach, turns his head to the side, checks his pulse, and looks at me, as if assessing my competence. "You take that wound." He points to the one closer to his shoulder. "Put direct pressure on it. Lots of it. Don't be afraid to lean your body weight against him if the blood keeps flowing."

He does the same on the second wound. When he is satisfied that we're doing all we can, he asks for a rundown.

I start with the sound at my window. There's no time for history. Before I'm finished, the second officer comes up saying that the area is clear. Douglas has escaped again. I want to scream. I grit my teeth instead.

Robe-clad, my parents appear as the EMTs arrive, and I realize how little time has passed since that first scratch at my window.

"What's going on?" Dad asks.

"Geoff's been stabbed!"

The EMTs ask us to step aside as they take over Geoff's care. I hear "loss of blood," and "in shock." They pressure bandage his wounds. Then, after sliding him onto a stretcher, they cover him with a blanket, put an oxygen mask over his nose and mouth, and carry the stretcher to the ambulance at a coordinated pace. They pull the back door closed, and drive away with lights and siren splintering the night.

"You did fine. We got to him quickly enough that he didn't lose too much blood." The officer takes both my bloody hands in his, and looks into my eyes.

"I must get to the hospital. He'll need me when he wakes up—and I want to be there while he's in surgery." I push past the cop to my car, but I stagger dizzily. My vision goes spotty.

"Steady there." The officer eases me down to the ground. He squats beside me, supporting me. "It's up to the medical specialists to figure out what internal injuries he has. I imagine there won't be news for hours, so clean up and get some sleep, if you can. You'll just feel helpless if you stay up and wait. You can check on Geoff later."

"No. I have to go." I push down on his shoulder and manage to get myself standing. In about 20 seconds, the spots are fluttering before my eyes again and I groan and sink back down. My body refuses to obey my need to follow Geoff.

The other officer has been talking to my parents, who now come over to me. We are all hugs and tears as they help me back inside and into the bathroom. My mother takes a look at all the blood on me. "Are you sure you're not hurt, sweetheart?" Her face is pale and stretched.

"No, it's Geoff's blood." I spread my arms away from my sides, looking at my ruined clothes and sort of glazing out. I want to chase after the ambulance, but I really need to lie down. My knees quiver, my body trembles and I bite my lip. Then I put my head down between my knees to stop the room from spinning.

"Are you steady enough to shower?" Mom asks.

I don't answer. My body is certain to betray me again.

"Can you stay here alone for a moment? I'll be right back." She comes back with a blue plastic stepstool and sets it in the shower. She helps me sit on it.

"If you can get undressed, kick your clothes into the corner of the shower and I'll take care of them later. I'm going to sit right here on the toilet in case you need anything."

She adjusts the water so it splashes onto my knees. "This has to be a terrible shock. You'll be better able to face it after you sleep."

"I can't sleep now. I have to get to Geoff!"

It's one of those times that Mom is one of the best parents ever. She must be dying to ask what was going on, but she just supports me. I do everything she tells me to do, and try not to think too much.

She walks me back to my room when I'm dry and helps me under the covers. I'm still on the verge of fainting.

"Mom, set an alarm for a couple of hours from now. I'm going to be at the hospital when Geoff wakes up. I have to be."

"Okay darling."

I let go of consciousness at last and fall into a deep hole.

* * *

When I wake up, it's already light. Way too much time has passed, but I don't know why that's important. It takes a moment to sort through my dreams back to the attack on Geoff. With a gasp, I sit up so fast that my head hits my reading lamp.

The knife comes down into his back—once, twice—and his knees buckle. I push the reading lamp out of the way, and it falls onto the floor. *Stay there.*

I rub my head and wonder whom to call. I must find out how Geoff's surgery went. But I don't know the hospital's number. I don't know whether Swedish Woodsdale is where they took him. He could be down in Seattle.

I grab my cell and speed-dial Geoff's number, even though I imagine the hospital crew has locked his cell away with his belongings.

But just as I'm about to hang up and ask my phone for the Swedish Woodsdale number, Geoff answers.

Although I managed not to pass out through all the fear and the blood and the horror of last night, the sound of Geoff's voice nearly makes me faint.

"Where are you? Are you all right?"

"I'm in the kitchen eating breakfast, and I'm fine. Tiegen, you sound ill. What's up?" His voice is the sweetest music I've ever heard.

For a moment, I'm unable to sort out my dream from my waking world. "You're home? You're okay?"

I hear him set something down and pull up a chair.

"Talk to me Tiegen. What happened?"

As soon as I begin the story, it all spills out in a deluge of emotions, assumptions and accusations. When I run out of words, Geoff finally speaks again, softly but with firmness in his tone.

"Hey hon, I'm right here in James' kitchen eating a muffin, not in a hospital. Nobody stabbed me. I'm just fine. You must have dreamed all that rot. I've been home all night. Queen's truth, there's nothing to worry about."

But I do. Because I have no idea which is the dream and which is real — that Geoff was stabbed by Douglas and is in the hospital, or that he's home and safe. Was I dreaming earlier or am I dreaming now? "I-I don't know if I'm awake, or what's real."

"Have you dreamed that you were dreaming before?"

"Yes, a few years back when Grandma died. I couldn't figure out whether she was alive or dead. It was insane. They had to hospitalize me until I could figure it out, but I don't remember much about the ward that time around."

"I'm on my way over to help sort it. Meanwhile, call Jessica. She'll know if the police were at your place last night. If your mom is up, talk with her, too."

"Okay. I'll call the police. But am I awake or asleep now? Your call might be the dream." A cavern in my stomach grows large enough to engulf me. There's no way I can tell.

"Just hold on until I get there, okay? We'll sort it, I promise."

Before I call the police, I go to my window. The screen is there: uncut, unbent. There's no sign that anyone has been outside: no footprints, no blood. So in this storyline, Jessica will say no police came out. But that doesn't help.

When I was little, my father would tell me to pinch myself if I thought I might be dreaming. If I felt it, I was awake. At the time, I trusted that he was right. But later I had a dream where I felt my fingers pinch my arm, even though it wasn't real.

I pinch myself now, though, desperate for data. I feel the pinch, whatever that means. I pinch myself again. And again. My arm reddens, but I'm just as confused.

Finally, I phone Jessica. She picks up on the first ring.

"Am I awake or dreaming? I can't tell."

"Tiegen? Tiegen, are you all right?"

"Were the police at my house last night? Was Geoff stabbed and taken away in an ambulance? If he's dead, my phone call got him killed."

"I don't think anyone came out to your house, but let I'll check the night logs. Just a minute." She clinks down the headset of her office's landline.

I stare at the window, expecting Douglas at any moment. I grab a book from beside the bed and hold it against me. It's a lousy weapon, but I feel a little more in control. It's a dissertation resource, thick and heavy — a shield that would stop his knife.

"Tiegen? There was no call to or from your house last night. No sign of Douglas or his pal, and no crimes that look like them either. Does that help?"

"I don't know. I might be dreaming right now, and Geoff died on the operating table last night. Everything you tell me might be a dream. Maybe my life is the dream, and my dreams are the only reality." My voice rises in pitch, so I bite my tongue and go quiet.

"Take a couple of deep breaths, Tiegen. You're mixed up—that's all."

I doubt they will help, but I take in two sweeping breaths. My head spins.

Then I hear the doorbell.

"Geoff's here. I'll talk to him." I hang up.

But that is all I can do. I can't get out of bed. Everything seems too hard—too unsure. What appears to be floor, beside my bed, might be a chasm. I could be sucked into a whirlpool and taken into the depths of the sea, where I'll die, fruitlessly filling my lungs with seawater.

I'm sure only of my bed, so I grab the duvet and pull it over my head while my mind closes down. I wait for everything to stop whirling.

I know how to wait.

Chapter 28

I'm in the wacko ward again.

I know because the bed is hard, I get pushed from room to room, and I'm fed hospital food. I do nothing for myself. Why bother? I'll never leave. My brain quit working, so others can think for me. I'll hang with my sister-by-association, the wheel-chair statue. We sit together in the activity room like bookends. If the rocking boy is here, he can hang out with us, too.

The three monkeys: see no evil, hear no evil, speak no evil. I'll be "think no evil." I simply won't think. There's something I don't want to remember, I know. But I ignore it. So there's nothing I need to do. Just sit here. Where I belong.

As I zone out, the nurse comes up.

"Time for your appointment with Dr. Crenshaw." Without waiting for a response, she wheels me down the hall to the doctor's office. I suspend my mind and wait. Time supports me.

The nurse wheels me inside and closes the door behind me.

I wait.

"Hello Tiegen. How are you today?" Dr. Crenshaw asks.

I let the words float around me like soap bubbles. Sparkly little baubles that soon pop.

"I see you still don't have much to say."

Pop. Pop. Pop.

"I'm going to ask a favor of you, Tiegen," the doctor says.

I see the rainbow in each bubble.

"You don't have to do this if it is way too hard for you, but I'd like you to give it your best try, okay?"

Light shimmers, then the bubble is gone.

"Will you please say something to me? Even one word would be great."

I watch the bubbles float and pop, float and pop.

"One word? Tiegen, say just one word for me, please?"

"Rainbow." There. Now I can ride the bubbles.

"Rainbow. Excellent. I'm pleased, Tiegen. That's the first word you've spoken since you came in—how many days ago was that?"

"Two." I hear the word, but I'm not sure which of us spoke it.

"Yes, that's right. I'm glad you know what's going on, even if talking is unattractive right now."

Bubbles juggle and bounce.

"Do you know why you're here, Tiegen?" Pause. "Tiegen?"

"Crazy."

"But you're not crazy, you know."

Until now, it has been easy conversation. No stress. But this statement tugs at me.

"Belong here," I let my mind, slip, slip, slip.

"For a little while, it's probably a good place for you. We'll help you get well so you can return home."

She is trying to make me think. I won't.

"Stay."

"Nobody lives here. This is a hospital, Tiegen. You are here because you decompensated. Do you remember what that means?"

I don't answer.

"It means you pulled back into yourself so you could heal. You've had a good rest, and now it's time to come back out again."

Lots of words. Lots of bubbles sparkle, quiver. I watch and turn off my ears. It takes time for all the bubbles to pop. Time is kind to me. It is serene.

"Your parents call every day and ask how you are. Would you like to see them?"

Somehow this reaches my ears, and I have to think about it. I miss Mom. And Dad. But the cost is so high. I can't go home, where dreams are a liability.

"Visit here?"

"We could work that out. Once you're talking a little more. I worry that they'd be concerned if you were silent. What do you think?"

I have no answer. This is who I am now. I'm already exhausted by all the words I've forced through my lips.

"Would you like to see Geoff?"

I try to let these words float away as bubbles, but I cannot. How odd. I touch my face and look at the moisture on my hand.

"What do you feel?"

"Geoff."

"What about Geoff?"

"Can't."

"You can't see Geoff or you can't talk about Geoff?"

Her questions pull at my protection, and I shiver. I look for the bubbles, but they are missing.

"Tiegen, what happens when you think about Geoff?"

I am crying harder. Can't she see? This is what happens.

"Why the tears?"

"Afraid."

"What are you afraid of?"

"Blood."

"Geoff's blood?"

I look away.

"Geoff isn't bleeding, Tiegen. He told us that you dreamed about him being stabbed. But that wasn't real. It never happened."

I look at her, wanting to believe her, but I can't tell whether this session is real or a dream.

"Are you real?"

"Yes. You are awake. This conversation is actually taking place."

"Prove it."

"That's the stickler, isn't it? How can you know what is real and what is a dream?"

"Can't."

"You used to be able to tell. You used your journal, your calendar. Remember?"

I remember, but I don't speak.

"You graduated—got your Master's. You couldn't have done that unless you sorted out your dreams from reality. You made a few mistakes, but not many. You overcame your disability."

"Flexman?"

"Who?"

I don't answer her.

"The police are watching the home of the suspect who tried to kidnap you, hoping he will turn up there."

"I led them wrong."

"They found the second suspect's name and address through the health club's file."

"That's real?"

"Yes, it is. Do you believe me?"

I think about it.

I realize I do.

* * *

My parents visit the next day. A nurse walks me into the visiting room where they both sit. I stop just inside the door. My stomach churns. I can't speak, and my eyes flood.

But Mom stands right up and comes over to me, holding out her arms, as sure about loving me as ever. I see it in her expression. Her eyes drown as well.

Dad is right behind her with that special smile he's always had for me. "It's wonderful to see you, Tiegen."

I know that's true.

"You too." Suddenly the silence falls away and I can speak again. But first they both hug me and hug me.

A few minutes later, Geoff comes in. I get out of my chair and hug him, too. How did I forget my life—the people I love?

I don't belong in a hospital. I'm only semi-crazy.

My life is good.

I'm coming back.

Chapter 29

Two days later, once I'm keeping up my journal and calendar again, Dr. Crenshaw encourages me to return home. I tire quickly, so I stay around the house. Mom and Dad give me lots of room, but are there whenever I need them.

Geoff keeps me company. I let him read my journal and he helps me "sort things," as he puts it.

It seems I had what most people would call a mental breakdown. When I thought Geoff was horribly injured, I couldn't accept it. That overloaded my circuits.

I can't be certain it'll never happen again, but Dr. Crenshaw says not to consider a trip to the hospital as a failure.

"Think of it as a place full of people who support your life in the real world. They help you get back on your feet when you need it. They're not jailers.

"Tiegen, although only you have this dream disability that we know of, you aren't so odd. Many people with mental illnesses don't fit diagnostic guidelines. It's difficult to categorize them. There's a lot that the field of psychiatry still must surmise about how the mind functions.

"The brain is complex. It's a miracle that it works as well as it does so much of the time for so many people. Count yourself lucky — people check in every day who never make it back to pre-breakdown functioning."

I guess the medical community keeps practicing, and the researchers keep studying, and the rest of us keep stumbling about while they figure out how to improve our lives. And that's basically all we can do together.

So I hug Geoff a lot, and tell my parents that I love them every day. I gradually get back into the things I enjoy: I geocache, take bike rides with Geoff, and read.

I will recover this summer.

I must.

* * *

Another week passes. I dig out the books I checked out from the U. They are tough reading at times, but I see an idea for my doctoral thesis materializing as I slog through them. I keep a separate notebook for my thesis, full of what-if's and question marks and quotes that encourage me to learn more. I scan and print out pages and sometimes chapters that I don't want to be without. I stay away from the library. Instead, at night, I read until I fall asleep.

One night, in bed, I find myself reading the same page over and over again with little comprehension. I sigh. *Time to sleep*. I slip a bookmark inside, and set the book on the floor beside my bed on a stack of others. No need to push it. It'll be here in the morning to tackle again.

Before reaching up to turn out my light, I stretch and yawn. Then I wiggle down under my covers and close my eyes, expecting to be asleep within minutes.

I awaken at the sound of a scratch at my window. My heart pounds and my eyes stretch wide, trying to pierce the darkness. Nothing moves.

I get up and pull the blinds part-way open so I can peek out, but I see nobody outside. The nightlight in the hallway reflects on the glass, and I move my head back and forth, trying to peer around the glare.

I stand for a minute, squinting into the dark, trying to hear anything beyond my thudding heart. I am reluctant to put my face up to the window where I can see better, remembering the dream about Douglas looking back at me like a monster.

But I shake off those concerns—that was, after all, a dream—and cup my hands against the glass to shade my window from the hall light. For a moment, I see little. The yard is steeped in shadows and only with difficulty can I distinguish the landmarks that I see during the day.

As I'm about to shut the curtains again, a figure steps out of the bushes and puts his face almost up to the screen. I gasp.

Just like before, it's nightmare Douglas.

Chapter 30

I run to the bedside table and grab my phone, but then I return and flatten my back to the wall with the window so Douglas can't see what I'm doing. As I dial 911, I ask myself if this is real or a flashback to the dream I had where Geoff was stabbed. The details differ, but enough of it jives, that I take another glance out the window.

Nobody is there.

The phone picks up at the other end.

"911 Operator. What is the nature of your emergency?"

"I just saw someone outside my window, though I don't see him now. Can you send the police out to look around the yard, just to make sure?"

"Of course. I show your address as..." She makes sure she has the information to find me. "Please don't hang up. I'll stay on the phone with you until the police arrive."

I'll do things differently this time. I won't call Geoff or my parents. Instead, taking my phone along, I walk into the hallway right next to my bedroom door. This is a tiny, semicircular niche that opens into three bedrooms: mine, the guest room and Mom and Dad's. From here, if he breaks the glass in my window, I'll have a chance to dash into a bedroom or the living room.

Then a thump sounds from the front of the house. I flinch. The sudden quickness of my breathing makes my vision swim.

I change my mind about waking my parents. I slip into their room and squeeze Dad's arm. "Can you come to the living room please?"

Immediately aware, from the tone of my voice, that something serious is wrong, he comes out in his pajamas, without bothering to put on his robe.

"Was it a nightmare, sweetie?" Dad asks.

I tell him where the noises were, and we listen together, his arm around me. We hear the fridge fan kick on and the house settle—nothing unusual.

I'm just about to shrug it off as nerves, when a thunk sounds at the opposite end of the house. It's nothing like the earlier sounds.

Dad puts his finger to his lips, and tiptoes toward the guest room.

Suddenly, in memory, I see the knife stab into Geoff's back, twice. I grab my father and pull him into the kitchen. "No Dad, it's not safe. Police are coming. Let them know what we heard when they arrive."

"I think he just cut through the window," Dad says. "Mom's in the next room. He could go after her. You stay here."

A voice speaks from my cell and I answer softly. The 911 operator says that an officer is pulling up to our house.

I hang up and look out the living room window. A uniformed man approaches our front door. I open it.

"You reported a trespasser?"

"He's more than that. This guy's wanted for attempting to set an explosion at Woodsdale Islamic Center. I was with the police when they thwarted him. Somehow, he's figured out where I live and come after me.

Before I called, I saw him at my bedroom window. Then I heard him in front. Now we think he's in back—maybe just cut through the guest room window." I point.

"Okay ma'am. Two other officers are in the car. While two of us circle the house after the peeper, one will stay with you near the front door."

"Please. No lights or noise."

He agrees, and vanishes into the darkness. He gets it that Douglas is dangerous, thank goodness.

I turn back to fill Dad in, but he's no longer in the kitchen. Pain radiates from the pit that is my stomach.

Hands on my tummy, I step into the hall niche. Dad is in the spare room, caught in a neck hold with a gun to his head. Whimpers form in my throat, and it is all I can do to hold them back, hands over my mouth, as I turn and run for the front door. I throw it open.

A surprised officer stands with his fist raised to knock. I pull him inside and left, to the kitchen door, and out of sight of the hall niche. On tiptoes, I whisper about Douglas and Dad. Squeaks slip out around my whispers, like blood spurting from a wound. I squeeze my eyes shut, then open them again.

The officer takes out his gun.

"Go into the kitchen." He gestures with his gun hand. "Hide if you can."

My eyes widen, and I nod.

He slips into the living room, gun in both hands, and moves toward Dad.

I go into the kitchen, but see no place to hide. My mind fills with fears for Dad's life, overlaid with memories of the knife stabbing and stabbing. The room spins as I struggle for clarity. I mustn't lose my grasp on reality. I bite my lip, and the pain helps me focus.

Inching open a drawer, I grab a carving knife. Then I creep back to the kitchen doorway. I listen.

Suddenly, a woman's voice, not my mother's, snaps, "Drop the gun and put your hands up. If anything happens to the man, you die. Let him live, and we'll talk after we take you in."

I scuttle into the living room and squat down low, peeking around the door frame, through the hall, toward the three bedrooms. In the niche stands the officer who entered through the front door, his gun on Douglas. The woman must be behind Douglas and Dad, because I can't see her.

Douglas raises his hands. Dad turns and runs past the officer in front of me. I jump up and hug him, then keeping an arm around him, I lead him back to the kitchen.

"Are you okay?" I look for blood on Dad, but he seems okay. I hug him again. "I was so scared!"

"I know sweetie. I'm fine."

"We're supposed to hide here." I say this even though I obviously haven't done so. I step back, and Dad jerks at the sight of the carving knife I'd held behind him. "Um, I thought it was better than nothing." At that, he surprises me by crossing the kitchen, opening the drawer, and grabbing another large knife without a word. I stand a little taller.

"Drop the gun," I hear the woman officer spit. I realize I never heard it clatter on the hardwood floor. Then a gunshot echoes through the house, followed quickly by a second one. I'm shaking.

I step toward the confrontation, but Dad catches my shoulder and whispers, "stay here."

"What's wrong? Who shouted?" Mom's voice quavers. Then come sounds of a scuffle. Dad lets go, and pushing me behind him, rushes back toward the hallway, knife poised.

"It's okay, dear," Dad calls. "Just stay in your room." His voice trembles.

Then a radio hisses, and the police woman says, "Send an ambulance and backup. I have one officer shot and the shooter in custody."

After that, I follow Dad's voice.

The male officer leans against the wall while one arm dangles weakly at his side. Blood streams from a shoulder wound. But his gun hand aims at Douglas, who kneels on the floor, hands behind his back. The woman officer snaps on his handcuffs. The third cop stands outside the guestroom window.

"Look at that! It's not the first time we tried to tie this guy down," she says, and I see another set of handcuffs: one end encircling Douglas' wrist, the other duct-taped to his upper arm.

"They're St. Marie's." I remember the dark-haired little girl with a pink ball.

The woman studies me closely. "That right? She's one good cop. I'll clean up this piece of crap for her." She gestures to Douglas at her feet. "St. Marie and I worked a few cases together when I was on days."

Douglas moves like he might stand up. "Remain on your knees. Hear me?" the woman orders.

He grunts, but doesn't speak. He quits moving, though.

My dad passes the scene and enters the master bedroom. He speaks softly to Mom, and then I hear cloth tearing. I run to the bathroom and grab the bandage tape.

When I return to the injured officer, Mom has dragged up a chair for him to sit on and she binds his shoulder with strips of a bedsheet. I hand Dad the tape, and he tears off long strips for her.

"Can you hold some pressure on that?" I ask. The male officer's blood seeps through the binding.

"No ma'am. Not and keep my gun on the prisoner." His voice is gruff, his eyes focused on Douglas.

"Go ahead. I've got him under control," the woman says. "Take care of that wound. I don't want to have to work with a rookie partner."

"I can either take the gun or hold pressure on the wound," Dad offers.

"I prefer to retain control of my own firearm, sir." So Dad steps up behind him and squeezes the heels of his hands against either side of the wound. Despite his injury, the stone-like concentration of the injured officer keeps his focus centered on Douglas.

By the time the ambulance arrives, the officer's whole body trembles.

Epilogue

The police pick up Baldy in the morning. He doesn't resist.

Jessica St. Marie calls to let me know it's all over. "He seems relieved that his friend is jailed and his role in the crime is finished. We found no sign of explosives at his place. He doesn't even own a hand gun. It was only after Baldy responded to Douglas' phone call for assistance, that he realized his help would break the law—at least, so he claims.

"He has a chance for a good plea bargain, if his involvement in the kidnapping was his only contribution to the scheme. He says he'll provide evidence against Douglas.

"It was Douglas who built explosives in his garage. The fertilizer was part of his recipe. He had timers, including one attached to those explosives in his van near Woodsdale Islamic Center."

Not surprisingly, Baldy's car contained an abundance of evidence showing that Geoff and I, as well as the two men, had been inside. And the security guard at the mini-storage described how he found Geoff, bound, inside the storage unit registered to Douglas.

In Douglas' house, the crime scene team found photos of Woodsdale Islamic Center and sketches of his bomb placement plan.

"Had he not been stopped," Jessica says, "the explosion would have devastated the Muslim community. Multiple deaths were certain considering the attendance at the center that night. You and Geoff kept harm from happening.

"Douglas won't get back on the street for years. He's charged with kidnapping, assault, breaking and entering, and creating an explosive with intent to kill. You won't see him at your window again.

"I'm proud of you." I'll write you a letter of recommendation if you decide on a career in police work."

I laugh. "I'll think about it." She really means it. And she kept my disability out of the case—protected me from stigma.

But rather than waiting all the time, I'm ready to live. I need to throw a lot of hours at my dissertation prep for a couple weeks to make up for getting behind. But I can do that.

No problem.

* * *

The day after Baldy's arrest, Jessica asks Geoff and me to join her along with the leaders of Woodsdale Islamic Center. It is a warm summer day, typical of the Pacific Northwest, with flowers blooming against multi-layers of green.

Officer St. Marie takes the lead. "At great personal risk, these two graduate students managed to do what the Police Department could not: they overheard the first stirrings of a plot, kept tabs on the suspect, and gathered evidence that allowed us to stop the crime before anyone could be hurt."

One of the leaders of the Islamic Center speaks next. "Thank you for saving our people. You are heroes to us." It's hard for me to take it all in. Heroes: a foreign grad student, and a disabled dreamer.

Life can be peculiar. Although I know that my dreams were as much a roadblock as a help, habits of observation, cultivated during years of testing real against unreal, may have contributed to picking up on the original threat.

"Hold that as one of your affirmations," Geoff says, "for times when you think you're crazy."

It's not a bad idea.

So, the Muslim leaders treat Geoff and me like geniuses, even though it was Jessica and Peter Landsbury who kept Douglas from planting his bomb. They tell us to consider ourselves as extended family. Several invite us to their homes, and they welcome us to their meetings. I have to admit, whether we deserve it or not, it feels fantastic to become part of a new community.

And Geoff, dear sweet Geoff, looks at me through eyes full of devotion when we're together, later. Instead of my flaws, he focuses on my strengths. It's like I'm a successful rancher instead of a cripple who can't keep reality from twisting up like the tangled legs of a new-born calf. He tells me he hardly needs cannabis anymore, he's so at ease when we're together.

Scenes from the dream where Geoff was stabbed still haunt me, but Dr. Crenshaw is helping me work through that part. Once she heard the whole story, she sifted out the gains I'd made because of it. She even thinks my breakdown made me stronger.

Later this summer, Geoff and I will travel to UDub together and look for an apartment to share next year. Since he'd planned to get one anyway, he's going to pay for it until I get my finances straightened out.

Afterward, there are three National Parks, one with geo-caches, within a couple hours of home. We can camp in a tent for two.

Ah, privacy.

I can hardly believe my luck. If I hadn't come home for the summer, I never would have met this cocky Brit. That thought is more painful than the memories of the dream attack by Douglas. Especially when we're holding one another close.

The coming year should be a success. And who knows—maybe the rest of my life as well. I'll take on that image of myself in the mirror, and with the help of my loved ones, step out with faith in my abilities.

"One never knows where miracles shall occur." Geoff tells me this when we're finally alone again. "You're mine, my brilliant dreamer. And I love you." It's the first time he says it outside of a dream.

"I love you, too." We kiss like we'll never stop. Maybe now, we won't have to.

I wonder if being with somebody I love might allow me let down at times—not have to examine every minute of life so carefully. Imagining it, I get the shivers. Or maybe that's his lips on mine.

It appears that Geoff's right. Miracles really can happen anywhere and to anyone.

Even to a half-crazy grad student in Woodsdale, Washington.

A Note from the Author

I hope you've enjoyed reading DREAM MIRE. It was a joy to write!

As an indie author, getting my work out into the world takes an enormous effort. These days, an author's success can be made or broken by the number of reviews they receive on their works. These reviews are our bread and butter.

If you are willing, I would much appreciate an honest review on Amazon, Instagram or Goodreads. Tell others what you thought of Dream Mire so they can decide whether it might be something they'd choose.

My previous book, KILN ZONE also takes place in Woodsdale, and features a few cross-over characters in the police department. I've included the first two chapters, here, so you can taste the story! Just turn the page, and get ready for deep suspense.

Should you wish to reach me, you can find me on Instagram as Pacific NW Author, or on Facebook as Sharman Badgett-Young. I enjoy hearing from my readers.

Thank you so much for your support.

KILN ZONE

A Woodsdale Novel

By Sharman Badgett-Young

Thank you to my editors for increasing the quality of this novel.

To my mud-families,
past and present.

kiln *noun* \\\'kiln, \'kil\\

An oven, furnace, or similar structure, able to be heated to a temperature that will burn, fire, or dry out materials.

Chapter 1

Marca Ruiz rose, smeared in mud from her breasts to her knees — her badge of achievement.

A four-foot urn reared from her potter's wheel. She hugged herself and felt the stretch in fatigued muscles. Bottom to top, she'd pieced together three thrown segments of clay, smoothing the joins until the composite pot appeared as if crafted in a single pull. Since beginning ceramics in college, she'd taken eight years of practice to reach this point. The urn was her masterwork.

She scanned the other potters in the studio, focused on their own creations, and kept her victory dance internal for now, not to disrupt their concentration. But oh, she wanted to crow!

Lisa glanced up under Marca's gaze. "My God, Marca." She circled the wheel. "Wish I could throw like that." Her arm outlined the urn's shape in the air, curving like a belly dancer.

Others rose at Lisa's exclamation, surrounded Marca, and admired the curvaceous pot. At their praise, Marca's feet rebelled, pirouetting an exuberant arc. She grinned till her mouth hurt.

"It's inspired. Only, look at all the clay on your clothes, you poor thing!" Kit, another hand-builder, held a carefully assembled coffer in front of her immaculate apron.

Marca swallowed a giggle.

The group parted for Dr. Tim French, resident artist, and Dr. Matthew Fyre, Washington State's eminent ceramicist and the leader of this two-week workshop. The friendship between the two men, since Tim was Matthew's student in the 1980's, enabled Tim to set up the class—a coup for Woodsdale's studio of mostly unknown artists. Marca knew that Tim, in his forties, single and childless, saw the potters as a family of choice. She felt the same.

Matthew entwined his fingers, rested them on his stout midriff, and studied Marca's structure. "Masterful. You embraced my process and personalized it. Next week, we'll explore glaze techniques for sizable pieces. Promise me, if your urn is unfinished when I leave, that you'll e-mail a photo when it's complete. I must see what you do with it." He raised his palms and smiled at her.

"I'd love to." Marca beamed, swaying from foot to foot. On impulse, she pinched herself surreptitiously, and gave a low chuckle when she felt the pressure. *Yep, for real.* It was a heady experience.

She pressed a wire tool tight against the bat and cut beneath her urn. The pot, on its bat, fit on a drying-shelf beside the exit to the kiln shelter. She swathed it in overlapping sheets of dry-cleaner's plastic. When leather-hard, she'd trim the foot to complement its voluptuous line.

As others cleaned up, Marca rinsed her drip tray, dumped her slop bucket, and sponged down her wheel. Only Matthew still worked, sorting pieces by dryness for tomorrow's firing.

"See you Monday, mud people," Marca called from the door.

Alone Saturday, Matthew Fyre swung wide the gas kiln's door. Shelves waited, stacked just outside, while those from a previous firing formed a base inside. He hadn't fired this model before, but knew its type. Tapping a button, as a test, he nodded when the cone settings altered.

His shove glided a flatbed cart forward, heavy in his hands. He parked it against the wheel nearest the door where he could reach both it and the greenware needing transport.

Flipping open readers from his shirt pocket, he squinted through them. His notes mirrored his memory—a standard cone 04 bisque for a high-fire clay body. He turned the page.

A footstep sounded behind him. *Good, a helper from the class.* He smiled, but delayed a moment to scan his final notes. Then he straightened, about to turn in welcome.

But an elbow crooked tight around his throat from above and behind. His teeth clipped his tongue. His strong hands, by instinct, flew up to protect his windpipe.

He teetered backwards, tasting blood. A foot jammed into his heels, and stopped his step back to halt his fall. Toppling, he felt himself maneuvered toward the exit.

Five-foot-ten and in his sixties, he was at a disadvantage to this taller assailant. Still, after a life engaged in the physical work of a potter, one known for his massive pieces, Matthew was stronger than average.

He flung out his right hand, trying to seize the doorjamb, as his left continued to pry at the constriction against his throat. He hit a soft object, plastic covered, and then flailed wildly before knocking knuckles against the wall. Twisting his wrist, he scrabbled his fingernails against it, creating a high-pitched scritch as if scraping a blackboard, desperate for a handhold.

Then, viselike, his fingers crimped onto the molding around the door as his foe strained to tug him through it. The ceramicist's grasp slowed the attacker for several moments until his fingers wrenched free of the doorframe in a jolt of pain, fingernails ripping.

The attacker hauled him outside and Matthew snapped his right hand back to struggle at his throat. His eyes bulged and he battled for air, mouth open like a fish on dry land.

Using his Vietnam training, Matthew altered tactics. He bent his knees into an abrupt squat. The attacker's weight balanced, for the most part, on a single leg after his twist dislodged the potter's grip. Now, surprise won out. Matthew's weight pulled them down until both were off center.

The arm around Matthew's neck loosened, and he sucked sweet air deep into tortured lungs. The two tumbled to the ground, entangled. Matthew pushed the constricting arm up, over, and behind his head in one precise motion.

Shaking free in a jet of energy, he shoved powerful hands against the patio. Exploiting his upward momentum, he leapt ahead, sprinting before he stood upright, fingers pressed together, hands cutting the air at his sides like blades.

Five steps into his flight, a tackle from behind pulled Matthew's legs out from beneath him and knocked him forward onto the ground where his white-haired skull bounced like a coconut against the concrete. Rolling over, dazed, he struggled to focus on his assailant, one knee bending as he used his foot to shove his body backwards, away from the figure. His stomach roiled at the motion of his head.

Matthew gasped aloud. His first glimpse of the visage before him made his skin erupt into gooseflesh. Mouth gaping, the face lunged forward and pulled back as its hands snatched at him, a Halloween ghoul whose features stretched into inhuman lines. A bulky coat masked its body contours, but its lithe counter-movements seemed like those of a person half his age.

He wondered for an instant if a supernatural being had clambered out of hell to suck away his life force. Then he comprehended what his blurry eyes had seen. The features, and the cap of black hair, appeared misshapen because he viewed them through a nylon stocking that the assailant wore over his face.

Matthew pushed himself back again, still too dizzy to stand but scrabbling to stay clear of swinging, muscled arms. His fingers happened upon a chunk of brick behind him on the patio. He hurled it towards the blot of the spook face above him with all the coordination remaining in his shoulder and arm. Simultaneously, however, the assailant launched a fist at Matthew's head that his instability kept him from blocking.

The impact vaulted Matthew through fractured light into a dark tunnel that closed in on him, swallowed him, left nothing at all.

Chapter 2

Marca spent Saturday at home, catching up on chores set aside in favor of Matthew's ceramics workshop the previous week. But Sunday, as she prepared to attend her weekly book club, she couldn't locate her wallet. She searched the house twice before sitting down to focus her brain on where she left it. Last she recalled, she'd stuffed it inside her pottery locker on Friday.

Shaking her head at her forgetfulness, she hopped into her red Honda Civic and drove to the studio. The view of the Olympic Mountains against the sound couldn't salve her anxiety at having no driver's license along.

Matthew had promised he'd bisque fire every piece he could pack into the kiln. That must mean the majority, if not all of their pots. She'd pick up her wallet and sneak an early peek at the greenware shelf in the same trip.

A studio regular, she used her own key and let herself in through the front door to the ceramics lab. A metallic tang in the air suggested a firing underway.

Her gaze swept the greenware racks. The shelves still looked crowded. *How strange.* Every pot she hoped to deco-

rate remained in the studio, unfired. Her eyebrows wrinkled. *What happened?* She'd have to glaze items she'd thrown
and bisque-fired prior to the workshop, instead.

Entering the adjoining room, she read the labels on the
buckets of glaze Matthew had mixed especially for the artists. Turmeric Poppy. Earth in Bloom. Sapphire Satin. The
names excited her imagination. *I want these colors on my new
pieces, not my old ones.* Her mood chilled further.

She saw Matthew's notebook, open to instructions on firing the gas kiln. Tim and he must have a reason for their altered plans. She took a deep breath and exhaled it, helping
herself relax. *If this is the worst that occurs this week, I can com-
promise.*

Noticing the time, she grabbed her wallet and slammed
her locker. The studio door swung closed and she relocked
it. She visualized herself replacing her disappointment with
anticipation for her meeting, a technique she'd learned years
before. No way was she about to let unglazed pottery spoil
another moment of her day.

* * *

On Monday morning, Marca arrived at the workshop
about a quarter-hour early. Approximately half of the partic-
ipants had beaten her there and set out their projects on the
long wooden tables that stretched across the center of the
room, facing the garden view out the wall of windows. She
figured that, like her, they valued each minute of Matthew's
instruction, and didn't want to miss even a casual suggestion
from the master before class began.

"Greetings mud people," she called out. Voices echoed in
return.

Lisa hugged her. "Gotta do this now. I'm not going to
hug you later, if you're all squishy again." She grinned. "I
have my limits, mud woman."

Lisa built by hand using a decorative knack that Marca
envied. Unicorns, rendered in under-glaze, rampaged across

the pentagonal box she had constructed for her niece. They looked real—or would if unicorns weren't imaginary. To keep it out of the clay, Lisa wore her light-brown hair pulled back, revealing a porcelain complexion. Lisa's beauty exuded from inside and out. However, hand building didn't jacket the younger woman with wet slip. Marca viewed herself the luckier of the two.

Marca laughed. "I bet it all started during childhood. Maybe my mother didn't let me stomp enough mud puddles. So now I make up for all the fun I missed by taking my clay baths."

"Oh, you. So deprived." Lisa gave her a playful shove and they chuckled together.

"Were your pieces in the bisque fire this weekend?" Marca asked. "None of mine made it. I checked on Sunday when I stopped by and rescued my wallet from my locker."

"Let's open up the kiln and find out."

"You go ahead. I'm dying to check on my baby." Marca nodded toward her draped urn.

With a mother's gentleness, she removed the plastic she had wound around its top and inhaled the after-rain earthiness. She laid her palm against its cool surface and tested the resistance of the rim. Later today it would reach the perfect texture for trimming.

She removed the remaining plastic, and her eyes were assaulted by an indentation the size of an apple that dominated its base. She let out a low, "Ohh." Knuckle marks, distinct in the moist clay, showed where someone had struck the pot a sharp blow.

"Hey!" Marca's voice sounded louder than she had planned. "Look at this gouge. Anyone know how it happened?" She directed the curious eyes of the potters to the depression with a flick of her hand.

She heard murmured comforts, many having experienced unexpected damage to wet pieces in the past. But everyone seemed clueless about whose fist had marred the urn.

"You're lucky you threw it recently. The blow would have destroyed a drier pot. I bet you can ease it out," Kit said, "so no one notices."

Marca scrutinized the imprint. "You're right, it's reparable. The damage just shocked me. But I can reach inside with a paddle and slap out the indentation." Skillful repair would leave, at worst, only a slight irregularity.

Still, it irked Marca that nobody confessed. She always owned up to her mistakes. Of course, the person may not have arrived yet, and an apology might ensue at any time. She harrumphed once to herself then consciously let go of her anger, unwilling to give it power over her.

"Oh no!" At the cry, Marca turned to see Lisa rush back into the studio. "The kiln is empty," she said. "Not one pot inside. And there's this inexplicable mound of sand on the bottom. It's uncanny."

Curious, Marca, Kit and the two Korean-American potters followed Lisa out to the sheltered kiln area. For over a decade, the gas kiln had served as the studio's workhorse. The status window indicated its last function: a firing that started Saturday morning and completed at the atypical temperature of cone 02.

The substance lay in a roughly crescent-moon shape on the base of the kiln where pots usually sat stacked for bisque firing. Marca picked up a pinch of the gray granules and felt coarse, sand-like grit when she rubbed her finger and thumb together. It didn't feel like clay at all. She doubted it would dissolve in water. The pile of sand spread the length of the shelf, heaped higher towards its center. She sniffed, but perceived no scent except for the dust that inevitably collected in the shelter.

A flutter of disquiet crept into her stomach. *Something sinister happened here.* She looked at Lisa, who frowned. She imagined her friend felt the same.

"Where is Matthew?" Lisa, looked around the kiln shelter as if he might step out of the wall like a genie from a lamp. "It's time for the workshop."

"Past time." Marca nodded at the kiln's timer. "He should be in the studio, now. Let's check."

All members had arrived and set up for the day, resuming yesterday's work. Matthew was still not there. Marca, glancing at the men, saw only the two male studio members.

A grandfather, Dave Miller, improved his throwing skills every week. He owned his own wheel and kiln at home, but joined the studio for the comradery. His tee shirt, lightly spotted with clay slip, showed a man holding a pot and read: *My wheels are for throwing.*

Burly Quentin Brenner, several years Marca's senior, had the sweet features of a younger man. His stilted gait, however, revealed side effects of long-term psychotropic medication.

Tim dashed into the room. "Sorry I'm late, everyone. Hope you started anyway." His head swung around as he inspected the room. "Where's Matthew?"

Heads shook negatively, and voices sounded I-don't-knows. Eyes flicked up to the clock before returning to projects underway. Matthew, who had come in early each day during week one, was already fifteen minutes late.

The reminder of Matthew's familiar routine did nothing to alleviate the queasiness Marca felt. It increased incrementally as she wedged her clay, filled a bucket with water, and organized her tools at one of the wheels. She surveyed the studio. Other than Lisa, nobody acted very disturbed. But then, the studio always radiated focused relaxation—a shelter from the craziness of the outside world.

"So, nothing got fired." Ju-Mie, the older Korean-American woman, turned her face to Marca as she paused from shaping a set of dishes at the next wheel.

Marca said, "No. Yet the kiln ran through a full firing cycle. It's odd."

216

"Should I sweep out the kiln?" Lisa's voice was soft as she leaned down toward Marca. "We need to load a bisque before we leave today, since nothing got fired over the weekend. I'd rather use the large kiln, considering how much work is crowding the shelves." She jerked her chin at the greenware.

"No, not yet." Marca was not quite sure why she hesitated. "I'll take a couple of photos first. With Matthew running so late, things feel off kilter. A few pics will make it easier to explain what happened when I describe it later." She rinsed her hands in her bucket and dried them on her pants, leaving muddy streaks, and then slipped her cellphone from her pocket.

Lisa looked relieved. "Something's wacko. I'd feel better if we documented the firing, just in case. Unless Tim knows what happened." The friends' eyes met, and together they went looking for Tim.

The slight man, frowning, spoke on his office phone. "You mean, even though his room was unused since Saturday morning, you didn't think to call anyone." Tim paused, listening. "I've heard that before, too, but I think it's an urban myth. There's no waiting period before you can file a missing person report. Doesn't the well-being of your customers concern you?" He paused again. "Yes, I suppose confidentiality is important." His scowl indicated the comparative weight he gave it.

"Okay, I'll call his wife in Spokane and see what she knows. If I find out more, I'll get back to you."

Ending the call, he rubbed his eyes with the heels of his hands. "I'm alarmed. No one has seen Matthew since Friday evening. The motel manager says his bed hadn't been disturbed since it was made up on Saturday morning."

"He vanished," Marca said.

"Seems so," Tim said. "Hold on, though. There's one more call that might clear up the situation."

The two women stayed in his office instead of offering Tim privacy. But Marca sensed they were bound together in this potential catastrophe. Perhaps Tim felt the same, because he beckoned them to sit.

Marca's muscles tensed tighter and tighter during the phone call. Though she couldn't make out the words, she heard the volume of Alice Fyre's voice increase as the call progressed. Alice, 16 years Matthew's junior, had been married to him for over 20 years. She wasn't taking his disappearance well.

Tim hung up.

"She last spoke to Matthew on Friday evening and was unaware that anything was amiss before my call."

He drew in a deep breath and then rubbed his face with both hands. "I don't know what to think. This is very unlike Matthew."

"That's not all that's strange, Tim. Saturday's firing was messed up in a major way. You have to come out to the kiln." Lisa's eyes grew wide. "We need your insight on what I discovered this morning."

After the coolness of the dark office, the bright sunshine made Marca squint. Summer weather had nearly arrived in Puget Sound. A cool Pacific Northwest breeze flowed past, as they walked toward the kiln shelter.

Lisa pointed out the peculiar settings and the kiln, nearly empty. "I tried to figure out what happened, but only managed to rule out a few possibilities. That matter's not clay or powdered kiln wash, and there's a scad of it. Nobody had a pot large enough to disintegrate into a pile that huge. And if a pot did explode, we'd see larger shards in a smaller pattern. Do you recognize this stuff?"

"Not offhand," Tim said. "Give me a minute here." He knelt by the control panel to the kiln and pulled up several mini-screens of reports on the weekend firing. "Cone 02? Matthew planned a normal bisque fire to cone 04 this weekend. Cone 06 to 04 makes sense for high-fire clay in a bisque, but 02 to 1 matures low-fire clays like earthenware. This firing doesn't fit the clay body he chose for us to use in his workshop."

"Maybe he made a mistake," Lisa said.

"Matthew knew his cone settings by heart back when I was in his class decades ago. And near the back door, I saw his notebook open to the page he wrote while we discussed the kiln and the firings that we planned. Considering his experience, and that he even consulted his notes, there is zero possibility that Matthew misfired this kiln. But somebody did—someone who didn't understand much about ceramics."

The women hazarded no opinions. Marca felt as confused as Tim sounded. So, while Tim took notes on the firing, Marca photographed everything, including the screens of information and Tim studying them.

Finished deciphering kiln screens, Tim stepped to the open door, and knelt to rub a pinch of the grainy substance between his fingers, just as Marca had. He confirmed the women's suspicions that, not only was it neither kiln wash nor clay, it wasn't any chemical he kept on hand for glaze formulation either. He sprinkled the material onto the palm of his hand and examined it closely, but had no more idea what it was than they had. He sniffed it, put a small bit on his tongue, and then spat it into his hand, where he mixed the saliva and sand together. It didn't dissolve.

"My best guess is that it's sand. But where was it gathered?" Tim frowned. "There's no taste of salt, which I'd expect if the sand came from a Puget Sound beach. In fact, it has no scent or taste. It's irregular, with larger particles mixed in—stone chips perhaps. But no sea matter. Nothing like sand near the ferry."

"This is too weird. We better call the police." Marca sounded certain.

"You're right. We need a professional." Tim nodded agreement. "Matthew is missing, a dozen of you paid a hefty price for his instruction, and this firing was irregular. The whole muddle makes no sense."

* * *

Officer Benjamin Mulback arrived about an hour later. The potters had spread out around the studio, building by hand, throwing or decorating their ware. The tranquil ambiance the studio usually held was absent, however.

Everyone seemed to wait for something, Marca thought, although she admitted to herself that they might simply be waiting for Matthew's call with a plausible excuse for his nonappearance. She knew better than to let her emotions run wild, but they kept fighting to take her over.

Tim led the officer into his office, and the two women followed.

"Please, tell me everything you know about Matthew's absence," the middle-aged Benjamin said as they sat down. He took his hat off his light brown hair, and set it aside. "May I record this interview?"

"Of course," Tim said.

The three potters shared what they had discovered about Matthew's disappearance—the unconventional firing, his notebook, and Tim's conversations with the potter's distressed wife and the motel manager. Benjamin jotted notes as they talked, in addition to his recording. Then he asked for the names and phone numbers of the studio potters, and Tim printed out a class list for him.

"I just remembered something." Marca said. "A pot I created Friday was damaged when I came in this morning. I can't imagine how it connects, except that it happened since I went home for the weekend. It could have occurred Friday evening, yesterday, or even this morning, though nobody admitted they knew about it."

Benjamin asked to see the kiln. Near the back door, he paused to examine Matthew's notebook, still spread on the table near the greenware shelves, and studied the urn briefly, jotting another terse note. He was thorough, and didn't dismiss the fist-print, but Marca could tell, from his manner, that the damaged pot didn't excite him.

At the kiln, Benjamin's gaze first turned to the control panel that Tim indicated. He showed the same amount of interest as he had with the urn. But when Benjamin looked inside the kiln, Marca saw his eyes open wide. He squatted down and studied the grey substance without disturbing it. He took out a tape measure from his pocket, and measured the length and width of the pile.

Then, he removed a jeweler's loop, and gazed at the grains under magnification for several minutes, scanning different sections of the sandy heap. He asked about the spots where the substance had been touched, and Tim and Marca admitted that the pinch marks were theirs. After another minute, Benjamin put his tape and the loop back into his pocket, his face inscrutable, and rose to his feet with an aura of command that Marca hadn't noticed until that moment.

He made eye contact with each of the three potters. "I want you to leave. Immediately. Don't touch anything—you could destroy evidence. Try not to step on any footprints on your way out.

"I no longer consider this a missing person report. It's officially a homicide investigation. I must secure the crime scene."

"Why, what's that stuff in the kiln?" The sick feeling in Marca's stomach tried to climb the back of her throat.

"I can't be certain, but my educated guess?" Benjamin looked at Tim. "It appears to be cremated human remains."

Tim's eyes opened round. He gagged once and grimaced, slapping a hand over his mouth. Then he dashed from the kiln shelter and spat into the dirt where a struggling strip of garden grew. Ignoring Benjamin's order to touch nothing, he wrenched around the handle above the tap. Lifting the hose, he rinsed his mouth, and spat again. Again. And again.

Kiln Zone is available in paperback from createspace.com, and as an e-book from Amazon in multiple countries.

About the Author

Sharman Badgett-Young has been an amateur sleuth since she read her first Hardy Boys mystery as a young tomboy. She started her first novel in 6th grade.

Over the years, her detective skills have paid the bills as a research analyst and a Marriage and Family Therapist. She combined her training in psychology with her research abilities to create Tiegen's dream disability.

In 2014, Sharman won first place in a non-fiction short story contest for Write on the Sound in Edmonds, Washington. She has completed four 50,000+ word novel drafts in consecutive Novembers, thereby winning NaNoWriMo in 2013, 2014, 2015, and 2016.

Sharman resides in the Pacific Northwest. When not writing, she spends rainy weekdays at the pottery studio, rainy weekends combing the woods for hidden geocaches, and rainy nights curled up with her husband.

Made in the USA
Charleston, SC
28 November 2016